IMPOSSIBILIA

Aurora Award Finalist for Best Collection

"Rarely have I seen such an apt title to any book! Douglas Smith has given us three amazing stories that are so unusual and beautiful that no other name than Impossibilia could possibly describe this collection. Each tale was rapture and ecstasy, magical and mysterious, perfect and implausible. In short, I loved them all from the first word to the last. …READ THIS BOOK!!!"
—Mass Movement Magazine

"The writing is superb. Douglas Smith is an artisan and his stories beautifully crafted. …In my search for the perfect short story, the three in this volume certainly qualify."
—SF Crowsnest Book Reviews

"Both thematically and stylistically, these stories sometimes recall the work of better known authors, including Harlan Ellison, Theodore Sturgeon, and Ray Bradbury. But Smith puts such a personal stamp on his stories, and invests them with such depth of feeling, that they transcend the dangers of…imitation and emerge as wholly original. …There is a certain exhilaration that comes from reading the book's complex and powerfully emotional stories couched in that deft and smooth prose. …[Smith deserves] to be known to by a very wide audience indeed."
—Dead Reckonings review magazine

"Highly, highly recommended."
—Fantasy Book Critic

"The stories in this collection reach from van Gogh's rural France to the classic travelling fair to the far lost forest, and from timeshift to shapeshift to the activity of luck. That's range, or at least a glimpse of range, in the grand manner that harks back to Bradbury and Sturgeon and Ellison"

—*Chaz Brenchley, award-winning UK writer*

"A fun romp that delivered something different [with] stories that are exhilarating, enjoyable, and well above competence."

—*Speculative Fiction Reviews*

"A book that ably demonstrates what Smith is capable of as a writer, added to which, anyone who references Springsteen songs in their titles is going to get the thumbs up from me."

—*Black Static Magazine*

"In the three novelettes that comprise *Impossibilia*, Douglas Smith [lays] bare the psychological and emotional fragility that motivates his characters."

—*The Fix*

"[The] three letter perfect stories behind the expressionist cover art admirably display Mr. Smith's considerable creativity."

—*Hellnotes*

"Stories with hope are stories I need. ...I would very cheerfully read more stories by this author. ...Worth reading: definitely."

—*The International Review of Science Fiction*

IMPOSSIBILIA

DOUGLAS SMITH

Lucky Bat Books

OTHER WORKS BY DOUGLAS SMITH

NOVELS

THE WOLF AT THE END OF THE WORLD (Lucky Bat Books, 2013)

COLLECTIONS

CHIMERASCOPE (ChiZine Publications, Canada, 2010) *Sunburst Award Finalist, Aurora Award Finalist, Bookies Award Finalist*

IMPOSSIBILIA (PS Publishing, UK, 2008) *Aurora Award Finalist*

LA DANSE DES ESPRITS (Dreampress, France, 2011) *Prix Masterton Finalist, Prix Bob Morane Finalist*

SHORT STORIES

"Spirit Dance" (1997) *Aurora Award Finalist*

"New Year's Eve" (1998) *Aurora Award Finalist*

"State of Disorder" (1999) *Aurora Award Finalist*

"Symphony" (1999) *Aurora Award Finalist*

"What's in a Name?" (2000)

"The Boys Are Back in Town" (2000)

"La Danse des Esprits" (2001) *AURORA AWARD WINNER (French translation)*

"The Red Bird" (2001) *Aurora Award Finalist*

"By Her Hand, She Draws You Down" (2001) *Aurora Award Finalist; Best New Horror selection*

"Scream Angel" (2003) *AURORA AWARD WINNER*

"Jigsaw" (2004) *Aurora Award Finalist*

"Enlightenment" (2004) *Aurora Award Finalist*

"Going Harvey in the Big House" (2005) *Aurora Award Finalist*

"Memories of the Dead Man" (2006)
"The Last Ride" (2006)
"A Taste Sweet and Salty" (2006)
"Murphy's Law" (2006)
"The Dancer at the Red Door" (2007) *Aurora Award Finalist*
"Out of the Light" (2007)
"Bouquet of Flowers in a Vase, by van Gogh" (2008) *Aurora Award Finalist*
"Going Down to Lucky Town" (2008)
"Doorways" (2008)
"Radio Nowhere" (2009) *Aurora Award Finalist*
"Nothing" (2010)
"A Bird in the Hand" (2010)
"The Walker of the Shifting Borderland" (2012) *AURORA AWARD WINNER*
"Fiddleheads" (2013)

SPECIALTY BOOKS
"By Her Hand, She Draws You Down": The Official Movie Companion Book (2010)

A complete list of Doug's published fiction is available on his website at smithwriter.com along with excerpts and reviews of his work. An excerpt of *The Wolf at the End of the World* is also included in the bonus section at the end of this volume. All of Doug's works are available as ebooks in a variety of formats.

Join Doug's mailing list at smithwriter.com/mailing_list to be notified of new books and stories, award news, and events Doug will be attending.

CONTENTS

The Hummingbird's
Attention
at the Flower

By Chaz Brenchley

What's it about, then, this story thing?
It's about range but focus, breadth but intensity. It's an art of contradictions. Or else you can express that as though literature were oxymoronic by nature—range *and* focus, breadth *and* intensity—in which case it's simply unreasonable, making demands that go far beyond what it is decent to ask…

Well, yes. I'm sorry, did that really need saying? Literature has always been the most scrupulous, the most specifically demanding of the arts. It calls for a marriage of style and content that can be neither forced nor arranged but has to be striven for, sweated over, cultivated like something as precious and rare as it is obdurate and slippery—and that's for starters, that's before it'll get into bed with you. Then it starts looking for flexibility, for stretch: for range, in other words.

Range is not (yet) exclusively the province of the short-story writer, but things are tending that way. Novelists

are bracketed too closely; having made a successful invest-
ment, publishers want more and more of the same thing,
whatever it was they and the reading public liked in the
first place. Try digging lead out of your silver-mine, and
they don't really know what to do with it; whatever its
intrinsic value, they're not set up to sell that. And retailers
like to know exactly where a book belongs, which shelf it'll
jump off: which generally to their mind means the same
shelf that your last books went on. It's a conspiracy of lim-
itations, a combination of fear-factors and urgent impres-
sions that leaves a novelist constantly aware of borders, of
boxing-in. Having so little invested in them, short-story
writers still have the freedom to reach, to leap, to embrace
genre but defy categorisation.

There are only three stories in this collection, and they
reach from van Gogh's rural France to the classic travelling
fair to the far lost forest, and from timeshift to shapeshift
to the activity of luck. That's range, or at least a glimpse
of range, in the grand manner that harks back to Bradbury
and Sturgeon and Ellison; that's the freedom that the short
form allows, the humming-bird's brief attention at this
flower and at this one and at that.

The humming-bird's brief but *intimate* attention. That's
crucial, that's the other shoe dropping simultaneously.
Range *and* focus. The humming-bird doesn't stay long, but
it is intent and purposeful. Short stories are by definition
short, but they are not—at least, the good ones are not—
casual or anecdotal. They matter, often more immediately
and more intensely than a novel matters. Novels can be
vaster than empires and more slow, they have time and

are welcome to take it; short stories are necessarily urgent: "nine coaches waiting—hurry, hurry, hurry."

Urgency is a focus in itself. So is style sometimes, the freedom—again, freedom—to experiment, to take risks, to play with language in ways that would never work within the broad landscapes of a novel. In this form, a story can focus on its own words. Chiefly, though, the proper study of mankind is man. The proper focus of a story, any story, lies in the characters that inhabit it. Which is why science fiction is never really about the rocketships, any more than crime fiction is about the clues; a true story is neither a manual nor a crossword-puzzle. However it dresses, literature has its great themes—love and death, largely—and its lesser themes, and they mirror the natural concerns of life.

Which is why, whatever the setting and whatever the mood, Douglas Smith's stories turn inward, on their characters. Not always in a kindly way—fiction is necessarily ruthless, or else it degrades into sentimentality—but these are, nonetheless, stories that treat with hope, and will not in the end deny it. Dues are paid, and life goes on: reaching, purposeful, intent.

Bouquet of Flowers in a Vase,
by Van Gogh

"To express the love of two lovers through a marriage of colors…To express hope by a handful of stars…"

—Vincent van Gogh, letter to his brother, Theo

The painting screams Laure's name at Maroch. He stares at it in disbelief, choking back his own scream.

It is a still life by van Gogh. This gallery in the Musée d'Orsay in Paris is devoted to Vincent. Beneath the painting, a still life now herself, Laure lies dead.

You should have known she would come here, my love, says a voice inside Maroch's head. It is a woman's voice, but not Laure's.

I should have known a lot of things, he answers silently.

Don't look at her, says the voice.

I can't help it.

The scrub team works on Laure. Maroch had sent for them when the museum's Director called him. He still has some pull at the Company.

Don't look.

Maroch pulls his eyes away as the team lifts Laure's slim corpse onto the body bag. Instead, he stares at the painting, which is like Laure in two very particular ways: it is beautiful—and it is impossible.

Beautiful. Against a dark blue background, an explosion of flowers overwhelms a white vase. Overwhelms the viewer, too. The flowers, mostly white and yellow chrysanthemums, seem ready to burst from the canvas, run wild over the frame, spill onto the gallery floor. Spill, like Laure lies spilled.

Impossible. This painting can't exist. But her body gives lie to that. He reads the plaque beside the painting:

> "*Bouquet of Flowers in a Vase*: This still life is not mentioned in van Gogh's letters and has puzzled scholars as to its place in his artistic production. Most certainly a late work and possibly the Museum's first painting from his Auvers period (May-July 1890)"

Yes, most certainly a late work, he thinks. *Very late.*

A sound like something tearing cuts the gallery's silence—the zipper closing on the body bag.

Something tearing—her life—my life.

Don't listen, says the voice.

Maroch stares at the painting as the Director comes to stand beside him. Pale-faced, she wrings her hands. "Horrible," she says, looking at the body bag.

Don't look, says the voice. Maroch stays silent.

Turning her back on Laure, the Director stares at the painting, as if by focusing solely on it, she can restore the gallery to normalcy, to its intended purpose. "Strange," she says.

More than strange, he thinks. *Impossible.*

She shakes her head. "I know every one of his works. I know them like my children, the ones in our collection more so. The provenance of each, where it is—storage, on display, on loan. I can visualize this entire room, every brush stroke, every color. Everything about every one, but…" Her voice trails off.

Maroch continues to stare at the painting, knowing what will come next.

She shakes her head again. "But not this one. This one, I have no memory of. None."

Give it time, he thinks. He almost laughs at that. Time.

"No memory of ever seeing it," she says, "or reading of it in any biography or in his letters to Theo. As if it never existed until I saw it hanging here today."

"Have you checked your records?" he asks.

She sniffs. "I tell you I know his works. This one—" She stops.

This one you can't explain, he thinks, *so you'll check again.*

The Director sighs. "I'll check our records again. Maybe I missed it. Maybe it's there."

It will be there—now.

She turns from the painting to watch the cleanup team lifting the body bag onto the gurney.

Laure is inside that, he thinks.

Don't look, my love.

"Is this matter over now?" the Director asks, as if a suicide was no more than a troublesome audit of their books.

"It's over," he says.

It's not over, is it? asks the voice.

No, he thinks. *One more thing to do.*

"And no one will hear about this?" she asks.

"No one," he says. *That I promise you, Laure,* he swears.

The Director sniffs again, then leaves him, running off, no doubt, to check the museum's records. The cleanup team wheels out the gurney with the body bag.

"Goodbye, Laure," he whispers.

Don't look, my love.

His phone rings. It's Karsh. "Maroch! Are you there?"

Part of me is. Part of me just left. "I'm here."

"Have you seen it?" Karsh is excited. Even for Karsh, he is excited.

Maroch stares at the painting. "I've seen it."

"Do you know what this means? What we have done? What you and your *petite conne* have done?"

Maroch looks at the bloodstained carpet where Laure had lain. "I know."

"We're going to be rich, my friend. We are going to be powerful. Rich and powerful."

No. No, we aren't. "Rich and powerful, Karsh."

"This changes everything!" Karsh cries.

Yes, it does, he thinks. But he says nothing.

"Maroch? Are you there? We need to meet."

Yes, we do. "When? Where?"

"The cottage in Auvers. At seven tonight."

"I'll be there."

Karsh hangs up. Maroch checks his watch. Three o'clock. The cottage is a two-hour drive from Paris. He still has time. Time to remember Laure. He moves on to the next van Gogh in the gallery.

The Café Terrace on the Place du Forum at Night—Arles, 1888. A café street scene. Tables sit half-empty. An island of light from the patio spills onto a cobblestone street, yellow-warm and yellow-bright. A few passers-by, a waiter clad in black and white. A cold night sky, black-blue and star-swarmed.

He looks at the date again. 1888. Before Auvers. He remembers another café, where it all began.

Before Auvers...

❦

Paris, May 2008. Two months ago. A warm night at Le Café de Deux Magots. A table by the sidewalk, rare as happiness. Espresso, bitter as memory.

Karsh was talking. Karsh was always talking. "It's easy money, Maroch," he said, lighting a cigarette.

It's never easy, my love, said the voice. *Don't trust him.*

I don't.

A young couple strolled by, their arms linked, the girl's green eyes on the boy's face.

Were we ever that young? Maroch wondered.

Once, she replied.

"Not interested, Karsh. I don't do Company work anymore."

"It's not a Company job," Karsh said. "You'd work for me. With me. And you're the only one I'd trust with this."

Maroch shook his head. "No." The young couple disappeared around the corner. Maroch sent a silent wish at their backs. *Be happy—while you can.*

We were happy, weren't we? she asked.

Once.

"One hundred thousand," Karsh said. "American."

Maroch turned back to stare at him. Two years since they'd last met, but Karsh hadn't changed much. Inverted triangle of a face, a little fatter. Sandy hair combed straight back, a little thinner. Small black eyes, still bright and hungry.

"What did you say?" Maroch asked.

Karsh grinned. "Or fifteen per cent. Me? I'd take the cut."

Get up. Walk away, she said.

"Cut of what?" Maroch heard himself ask.

You never listened, did you?

Karsh's grin grew. "Already have buyers lined up."

"Fuck your dancing. Buyers for what?"

The waiter passed by, long white apron, black pants, white shirt, black tie, one hand holding a tray of empty wine glasses. Waiting until he'd gone, Karsh took a glance over each shoulder, then leaned across the table.

"Van Goghs," he said in a hoarse whisper.

Maroch laughed. "Where would *you* get van Goghs?"

Karsh sat back, taking a drag on his cigarette. "There is much about me you do not know, my friend."

He's not your friend.

"It's what I *do* know that worries me. How many?"

"Don't know yet."

"You think your buyers won't be able to tell?"

Karsh shook his head. "No fakes. Real."

"Stolen?"

"Never been found." Another grin. "At least, not yet."

Maroch's hand began to shake. He put his espresso down to cover the tremor. "Then, how?"

You know how, she said. *That's why he wants you.*

"I've found a natural, my friend."

A viewer. He's talking about a viewer.

"I'm not doing it, Karsh."

Karsh wasn't listening. "She's the best I've ever seen. I mean, since you. You know, the 'you' you were before Elise…" He shrugged. "Before."

Before I died, he means.

Dead, but not gone.

Walk away, my love, whispered Elise.

"I just need you to design the protocols," Karsh said, "and then train her on them. She does the remote viewing—you just guide her through each session, record what she sees, and report to me. No har-vee for you." His accent made R.V. sound like "harvey."

Walk away.

"She's waiting to talk to you," Karsh said. He nodded at a table on the far side of the patio, against the wall of the café. "Her name is Laure."

Maroch turned. A slim brunette sat with her back to him. As his eyes fell on her, she turned to look at him, as if she had felt the touch of his gaze on her skin. Small rosebud mouth, short nose, large green eyes. Short hair, black and shiny, framing a round, pale face. Their eyes met, and she smiled. He gasped. The girl turned away.

Karsh nodded. "There *is* a resemblance."

Maroch swallowed, his mouth like sand. "I won't do any viewing."

Karsh shook his head. "None, my friend."
You're going to do it, aren't you?
Maroch looked back to Laure.
I need the money.
Liar.
"Twenty-five per cent, not fifteen," Maroch said.
Karsh grinned.
You're a fool.

⁊

Maroch moves to Vincent's next painting in the gallery, "Houses in Auvers." Thatched cottages with tiled roofs. A winding dirt road. Green roofs over blue walls. Blue sky over green trees and gardens run wild. These peasant homes sag and twist, like living things, part of the surrounding verdant jungle from which they seem to have sprung.

He reads the plaque:

> "In May 1890, against his doctor's advice, van Gogh moved to Auvers-sur-Oise, transferring his care to Doctor Gachet, an art lover himself. Van Gogh painted many of his finest works in Auvers during a feverish burst of creativity in his final weeks."

Feverish, Maroch thinks. *Like a man possessed.*
He was possessed—by love. As you were.
As I am.
Maroch remembers another cottage in Auvers.

⁊

Karsh turned his black van off the highway onto a paved one-lane. The sign for the exit had read "Auvers-sur-Oise 90 km." Maroch sat in the front beside Karsh, Laure in the back. Maroch could feel her eyes whenever she looked at him.

"Why Auvers?" Maroch asked.

Karsh winked. "I wanted somewhere where van Gogh lived and painted. Somewhere where you remote viewing types could still feel him."

"Why not Arles?" Maroch asked.

Karsh shrugged. "It was another option. But his Auvers period was extraordinary—so many works in such a short time. Seventy days, seventy paintings. And some gaps exist in his letters to Theo then, where we don't know what he was working on. If there *are* missing paintings, I think Auvers is the most likely period to find them."

"Beautiful," Laure said from behind them.

Maroch turned to look at her. *Yes, you are*, he thought. The soft perfection of her face still made him catch his breath—that and her resemblance to Elise. "I'm sorry?" he asked.

"His Auvers paintings. They are his most beautiful, his most...intense," she said, staring at the trees flashing past.

"Besides, Auvers is where he killed himself..." Karsh said. Laure shivered.

Can't get more intense than that, Elise whispered.

Stop it.

Maroch turned back to stare at the road ahead.

"...and he's buried there," Karsh continued. "That's got to add some energy to any viewing done here."

Because the dead have so much energy…

Maroch swore he could feel Laure shiver again.

"There are also the probe results," Karsh added.

Maroch scowled at Karsh, jerking a thumb at the back seat.

"You shouldn't discuss the probe results in front of me," Laure said. "I shouldn't know what other viewers have 'seen.' It might bias my perceptions, skew my viewing."

Karsh nodded. "Right. Sorry. Well, at least I can tell you the protocols we used. We sent the probe package to eight other viewers, all proven in other work with the Company. None of them had prior knowledge of van Gogh's life. We didn't want their viewing tainted by any educated guesses. All they received was the probe question and a world map, plus country maps as well to narrow down the location if they could."

"What was the question?" Maroch asked.

"It was 'If you could locate an undiscovered work by the famous Dutch painter in history known as Vincent van Gogh, where would you look? And if you could describe what you believe is there, what would it look like?'"

Karsh turned the van onto a dirt driveway flanked by cypress trees on both sides. The trees ended after about a hundred meters, and the driveway circled in front of a low stone cottage with a green tiled roof. Karsh pulled up in front, and they all got out.

"Renting it from a pair of Brits who use it in the winter," Karsh said. "You two are newlyweds on your honeymoon. You wanted Paris, but not Paris prices."

Maroch glanced at Laure, who blushed and turned away.

Do you remember our honeymoon, love? Elise asked.

All I have are memories.

I am more than a memory.

Are you?

"You won't be bothered," Karsh said. "I know your types prefer isolation from other minds when you're viewing."

Maroch looked around. Nothing but fields and trees for at least a kilometer, past which he could make out the buildings of the town of Auvers, dominated by a church steeple.

"L'Église de Notre Dame d'Auvers-sur-Oise," Laure said, following his gaze. "Vincent painted it as 'The Church at Auvers.' It hangs in the Musée d'Orsay in Paris."

"Which reminds me," Karsh said to Maroch, "I've arranged with the Director at the Musée. You and Laure have private access to their van Gogh gallery after hours. We're an hour from Paris by train, two by car." He opened the back of the van and nodded at two boxes of books. "On van Gogh. Biographies, the complete letters with Theo, lots of reproductions. Figured she might need them."

"*She* is standing right here," Laure said, walking up behind Karsh. She ran her hand along the spines of the books. "And she has read all of these." With that, she picked up her suitcase and walked towards the cottage. Maroch stared after her.

"Bedrooms are up the stairs," Karsh called after her as she disappeared inside. He looked at Maroch. "Plural. Two of them."

"She's okay with staying here alone with a complete stranger? And a man?"

Karsh nodded. "Says she trusts you. Obviously doesn't know you very well."

Neither do you, Maroch thought. He looked at the books again, suddenly realizing something. "Laure. *She* is why you picked van Gogh as the target."

Karsh nodded. "She's obsessed with him. I used her last year on a Company project, helping the Russians locate a missing general and some warheads. She's uncanny—the best I've ever seen. Well, since you. Grab that other box."

Inside the cottage, they passed through a small sitting room, sparsely furnished with a low table stained dark brown, a floor lamp with a torn shade, and two armchairs upholstered in a faded flower pattern. A door off the sitting room led to a tiny kitchen, painted yellow with an ancient wood-burning stove, a small sink, a modern refrigerator, two mismatched wooden chairs, and an unfinished oak table.

Maroch put his box of books on the table beside Karsh's. "What were the protocols on the Russian project?"

"Team of six viewers," Karsh replied. "Started with just the coordinates of the original site where the Russians had stored the warheads."

"Space coordinates only? Or time, too?"

"Just latitude and longitude to start. Asked them what they saw at that spot, and then stepped them back a year. She's the only one who 'saw' the warheads at the earlier date. Then we gave her a map to mark where the warheads were now. She led us to five of the six, plus she identified the city and described the building where the general was holed up. We found him and eventually, uh, convinced him to provide the location of the last one."

Maroch could hear Laure moving around upstairs. "Why van Gogh? I mean, with her. Why her fascination with him?"

Karsh shrugged. "Don't know."

He's lying, my love.

"But she's right," he continued, nodding at the books. "She probably won't need these. She knows more about van Gogh than you'll find in the lot of them."

"Tell me about your van Gogh probe results."

Karsh gave the ceiling a glance and lowered his voice. "All eight viewers came back with a scattering of cities in France, most of them focusing on Auvers, Arles next, then St. Rémy. All places where Vincent lived and painted."

"That's encouraging. Any images?"

"Inconclusive. Several reported a strong image of a particular painting that kept disappearing and reappearing, first clear and sharp, then gone completely."

"Did they describe it?"

Karsh nodded. "A still life. A bouquet of flowers in a white vase. Might not mean anything." He looked at Maroch. "So what protocols will *you* use?"

Maroch shook his head. "This isn't standard. I don't like using a single viewer…"

But you like the viewer being single.

"It works best with a team," he continued. "You can look for patterns, focus on aspects that all of them are seeing…"

Or hearing. Sometimes there are voices.

But are you real? Or imagined?

"That's not an option, my friend," Karsh interrupted. "A team means more people I have to trust to keep quiet. More people to cut in if we find something. That's why I brought in only you. You're the best, and I trust you. Besides, like I said —she's uncanny. She'll come up with more than any group you could put together." He looked at Maroch, waiting.

Maroch sighed. "We'll start by visiting sites in Auvers where he painted. Then I'll step her back to 1890—see if she picks up anything. If she knows van Gogh that well, she could look for paintings in his style she's never seen before."

Karsh nodded. "Sounds good. But you're the expert."

"Don't get your hopes up. I've never tried focusing on that specific a time period before. And we'll need a researcher, to check anything she comes up with."

Another nod. "I've got researchers and data analysts in Paris. Email me your notes. How long you figure?"

It was Maroch's turn to shrug. "No way to tell."

Karsh turned to the door. "Well, I've rented this place till the end of July. If you haven't come up with anything by then, we'll try Arles next. Or St. Rémy." He nodded towards the refrigerator. "You're stocked for a week. There's a Citroën rental waiting for you in town. I'll drop you back there now."

"You're leaving?"

Afraid of being alone with her? she asked.

Karsh shrugged again. "Something else you need?"

My sanity back, he thought.

You'd be even lonelier then.

Maroch just shook his head.

"Then let's go," Karsh said, and walked to the door. Maroch called up to Laure, telling her he'd be back in an hour. She didn't answer. He followed Karsh to the van.

Karsh grinned at him as they pulled away from the cottage. "Do me proud, my friend, and we will soon be very rich."

"No promises."

"Understood," Karsh said with a nod. "No promises."

In the gallery, Maroch moves on to the next painting.

No promises, Elise whispers. *But you made her promises.*

I made no promises.

Maroch stares at the scene before him. In "The Church at Auvers—June, 1890," the small stone church seems a thing alive, writhing in the bright yellow French sunlight, reaching for a deep azure sky. But the sun, though bright on the ground, is absent from that sky, a blue expanse that hints more of depths of darkness than heights of heaven. The windows of the church frame that same deep blue, as if the church contains, not pews and pulpit, but the sky itself, the same darkness.

He stares, remembering. That church had not been the only thing in Auvers with depths of darkness inside.

You made her promises, says Elise. *You made your first right there that day.*

I made no promise.

A kiss is a promise.

When Maroch returned with the Citroën, Laure was sitting on the stone step of the cottage, her face to the June sun.

She walked to the car and leaned in the far window. "I want to go to Auvers," she said.

Maroch tried to ignore how her breasts pushed against the soft cotton of her blouse. He hesitated. "We should research the town before we go."

Laure smiled. "There is nothing we need to know about Auvers that I can't tell you."

He considered that. "All right. But no viewing today. I haven't decided on the protocols yet. We'll just reconnoiter." He reached over and opened the door for her.

She shook her head. "I want to walk, as *he* walked." She headed down the tree-lined driveway, hips swaying more than he wished he noticed. He sighed, got out, and caught up to her.

As they walked along the road to Auvers, passing by the fields of Vincent's paintings, Laure would name each of his works that the landscape brought to mind. *Wheat Field under Clouded Sky…Wheat Field with White House…Wheat Field with Auvers in the Background.*

"He liked wheat fields," Maroch commented.

Laure stopped. She stared out at the fields glowing yellow under the hot sun. "'I am now quite absorbed by the immeasurable plain…immense as a sea…'" she said softly. "'I am in a mood of nearly too great calmness, in the mood to paint this.'"

He looked at her. "Vincent?"

She nodded. "He wrote that to Theo on July 27, 1890. Later that same day, he walked out into these very fields to paint as always. But he didn't paint that afternoon." She turned towards Auvers again. "He shot himself."

This girl is broken, my love.

He stared at her back for a second, then ran to catch up with her. They walked in silence for a while, Maroch trying to think of something to break the suddenly dark mood, until they reached a tiny cemetery just outside of town, surrounded by a high stone wall with tall iron gates.

Laure stopped. "Vincent and Theo are buried here." She turned to him. "I want to go in."

That should cheer her up, said Elise.

The cemetery was tiny, and they easily found the graves where Vincent lay side by side with his brother. Laure stood silently before the two simple headstones. A thick garden of ivy covered both graves, joining them under a single green blanket.

"The Catholic church in Auvers wouldn't let him be buried there," she said, "because he was a suicide. Theo died six months later in Utrecht, broken by grief, they say. In 1914, Johanna, Theo's widow, had him moved here too."

Laure plucked an ivy leaf from Vincent's grave and another from Theo's. "Johanna planted a sprig of ivy from Dr. Gachet's garden here—this very same ivy that now joins the two graves, a symbol of the bond of love that had existed between the two brothers in life." She tucked the two leaves inside her blouse, and he caught a glimpse of the soft curve of a breast. "A bond that even death could not break."

Turning her back on the graves, Laure began to walk out of the cemetery. But this time she stopped and waited for Maroch, smiling at him when he reached her.

A bond that even death cannot break, he thought.

Remind you of anything, my love?

They walked again in silence, but she had moved slightly closer to him. Laure nodded at the steeple of the church, now clearly visible. "His painting of the church hangs in the Musée d'Orsay. We'll see it when we visit the gallery." Strangely, the visit to the cemetery seemed to have lifted her mood.

Death is so uplifting.

"Have you been to Auvers often?" he asked.

She shook her head. "I could never afford the airfare."

He frowned. "I thought you lived in France."

"Montréal. I'm French-Canadian. If you were French, you could tell. The French here turn up their European noses at my accent, my idioms. You're Austrian?"

Maroch nodded.

"Karsh tells me you are a viewer as well. One of the best he's ever seen," she said.

His jaw tightened. "Was."

"Why did you stop? See something that disagreed with you?" she said with a laugh.

More with me than you.

Shut up, he swore silently. *Go away. For God's sake, go away.*

Never, my love. You need me.

Something must have shown on his face. "I'm sorry," Laure said. "I'm being rude. I didn't mean to pry."

"It's all right," he said. *It's not all right. It will never be all right.*

One day, my love.

They walked on in silence, and he felt her eyes every time she glanced his way.

When they reached the church, Laure walked back and forth in front of it several times before she was satisfied that she'd found the exact angle matching Vincent's painting. She stared at the church for a good five minutes before finally shaking her head. "It's just stone and glass and wood. He made it come alive. This is just a building. This is dead."

Dead, but not gone.

They went inside. The church was empty. They walked quietly to the front and sat in a pew, Maroch uncomfortably aware of her closeness, the heat of her body beside him.

"Are you religious?" she asked, staring at the cross behind the pulpit.

"Once," he said. "No longer. Not since my wife died."

You make it sound so simple.

He looked at Laure. So beautiful. So much like Elise. "You?"

She shook her head. "Once, as well. A lapsed Catholic. Ever since my father…" She turned to him then, looking into his eyes. He held her gaze.

God, she is beautiful, he thought.

Take care, my love. Beauty hides pain. Vincent knew that.

"He was an artist. He taught me to paint," Laure said. She swallowed, still looking at him. "He shot himself."

The penny drops, said his voice. *This girl is broken.*

She's in pain.

Pain and beauty. And that turned out so well with Vincent.

Maroch put his hand over hers where it lay on the seat of the pew, thrilling at the touch of her skin. "I'm sorry."

She left her hand there. "It was five years ago. My mother died when I was born. My father and I, we were very close. He used to call me his Angel."

"Why did he..." he began then stopped. "Sorry."

"It's all right," she said, dropping her eyes. "I ask the same question every day." She shrugged. "I don't know. He seemed calm, even peaceful before it happened."

I am in a mood of nearly too great calmness...

"It's why I began viewing. I hoped I could find him, in the past. Ask him why he did...what he did. It's why I became so interested in Vincent. So many parallels. So much written by him, about him. I keep hoping someone will solve the puzzle that is Vincent and in that answer, I will understand my father."

Your turn to tell secrets, whispered Elise.

"Laure, I—" Maroch began. He stopped and swallowed. The words would not come.

Coward.

Laure touched a finger to his lips. "No." She stroked his cheek. "No. I can tell you carry pain, but you do not need to tell me." Her hand continued to caress his cheek.

Pain and beauty. You make a lovely couple.

He turned his face until his lips touched her wrist. He kissed it. Her hand went behind his head, and she pulled him to her. Their lips met. He kissed her, softly at first then with a hunger, his arms around her, pressing her to him.

She smelled of flowers.

His fingers fumbled at the buttons of her blouse. She closed her hands around his. "No. Not here. Take me back to the cottage." He nodded. They kissed again and left the church.

On their way back, Laure stopped to stare as a flock of crows rose out of a wheat field. She shuddered. "It took him two days to die," she said, watching the birds rise into the sky like a storm-dark cloud. "Time for Theo to arrive, to be with him at the end."

Maroch was silent, not knowing what to say, hurt by her return to the morbid after their new intimacy, suddenly jealous of her obsession.

Why? asked Elise. *Did you think a kiss could fix her? Could fix you? You are broken, and so is she.*

"Do you know what his last words were?" she asked. "As he lay in Theo's arms?"

He shook his head.

"'La tristesse durera toujours.'" She turned from the scene. "'The sadness will last forever.'"

He swallowed. She moved closer. "Hold me," she said.

He put his arms around her, breathing in her flowered scent. "Your sadness will end, Laure," he whispered in her ear.

She looked up at him, a smile on her face that didn't reach her eyes. "As will yours."

But how, my love?

❧

Maroch moves on to the next painting. In "Garden in Auvers —July, 1890," the flowered plots are neat, the grass manicured, the paths raked, every edge precise. He thinks of another garden—the garden at their cottage—untended, grown wild, its paths hidden, choked with weeds and ivy.

Like you, Elise says. *Untended. Mind choked with memories. Your path hidden.*

But alive. It was alive. She was alive. You are dead.

Dead, but not gone.

He remembers standing in that garden and feeling its life, breathing its breath, heavy with the scent of spring blooms.

The scent of flowers.

*

She smelled of flowers.

Laure cried when they made love. Cried when he entered her, cried with each thrust, but so softly that he mistook it for sexual passion at first. He stopped when he realized they were sobs of sadness, but she only urged him on, harder, faster. After, he lay on top of her, fighting sleep as she stroked his hair. From somewhere, his words came.

"Her name was Elise," he whispered. Laure's hand stopped its caress. He swallowed. "We were both with the Company. I'd been in field ops."

Wet work. Tell her you killed people.

"I got injured. Nearly died. The company transferred me to a remote viewing project. I'd never done R.V. before, but my tests indicated an aptitude."

Laure nodded. "We all have the ability. Anyone can be trained. But with some—you, me—the talent is natural, stronger. Elise, she had that skill too?"

He shook his head. "No. She was field ops, but she worked with R.V. teams, so she was going through training when I was. We married shortly after that." *And they lived happily ever after,* he thought.

I was happy.

He had to force his next words out. "We were trying to locate a safe house of a suspected terrorist cell near Lisbon.

I was on the viewing team. We'd come up with very consistent results, pointing to a villa on the coast. Elise led the field team that raided the villa. I was worried about her…" He stopped, unable to go on.

"You tried to remote view the raid, didn't you?" she asked.

He broke down, burying his face in her breasts, sobbing. "I could see the scene so clearly. Through her eyes…"

"A psychic link focuses the power of a viewing—a link with that place or time, or with a person. The bond that you shared with Elise."

A bond you still share, my love.

Laure held him tightly, waiting for him to speak again.

"The team was ambushed," he said finally. "Elise was shot. Killed."

Laure tensed under him. "You still had the link."

"I felt her die," he whispered. "And I could do nothing." He lay there, trying to wash the death memories away with the sound of Laure's breathing, her heartbeat, the warmth of her body under his.

"She's still with you, isn't she?" Laure asked finally.

"I don't know, Laure," he said. "I hear her in my head. But I don't know if it's her—or if I'm mad."

So you finally said it out loud, Elise said. *Feel better?*

Raising himself on an elbow, he looked at Laure. "Am I mad? Is it her? Is she real?"

Laure stroked his cheek. "I don't know. Your pain—that is real."

And this girl knows about pain.

"I love you," he said, surprised that he meant it. He kissed her.

"Your sadness will end," Laure said between kisses.

But how?

They made love again. This time, Laure didn't cry.

When he woke, it was early evening, and he was alone in bed. He heard her singing outside in the garden. Rising, he washed and dressed and went downstairs.

Laure knelt before the low table in the small sitting room, arranging flowers in a white vase.

He kissed her neck then sat beside her on the worn rug. "From the garden?"

Nodding, she leaned back against him. "Do you like it?" The flowers were mostly white and yellow chrysanthemums, their pale colors contrasting with the dark green of leaves and stems.

"A pale bouquet, like you," he said. "So, yes, I like it."

She smiled. "It's not all pale. I used red. The color of passion, of love." She pointed to two chrysanthemums at the top right, close to each other but not quite touching. Their petals were mostly white, but tinged with red at the edges, as if they were blushing.

"Those two have just met," Laure said. "They will be lovers. Their passion—the red—is just beginning to show." She pointed to another pair, at the top left of the bouquet, all red and nestled against each other. "Those same lovers, their passion now aflame, their love declared." She kissed him. "Like us."

Maroch pointed to a single red rose in the center of the bouquet near the bottom. "What of that one? It looks so alone."

Laure shook her head. "Those same lovers still, their love now old and strong. Their younger passion has burnt away the boundaries between them. They have become one. Two hearts, one rhythm. Two souls, one journey."

I remember that rhythm, he thought. *I remember that journey. Still hear it. Still traveling.*

He tried to speak but his throat constricted. "I thought...I thought that they had lost each other. That one of them..." His voice trailed off.

Laure put her arms around his neck, laying her head on his chest. "You can never lose me, my love," she said softly.

Stroking her hair, Maroch stared at the single red rose. *It still looks so alone.*

You can never lose me, my love.

In the gallery, Maroch stands before "Village Street and Steps in Auvers with Figures." Here, Vincent shows a narrow street in the village sloping upwards to a set of steps that lead, he now knows, to the church that Vincent had painted. He counts the figures in this painting: five.

You, me, Laure, her father..., Elise says.

And Vincent.

It got a little crowded in there, didn't it?

The next morning, Maroch and Laure walked into Auvers again, this time hand in hand. They passed by the church, descending a set of steps to a street sloping down into town.

"Do you think this will work?" Laure asked as they walked.

Maroch glanced at her. This was the first time she'd mentioned the remote viewing project. He shrugged. "Schwartz used similar protocols successfully in Alexandria searching for Alexander's tomb. He started with a map probe then visited the most likely sites with the viewers who showed the strongest natural aptitude. And they went back over two millennia, not a hundred years. Yes, I think it can work," he said, "assuming there's something here to find."

"You're the expert. How do you want to proceed?" she asked as they passed L'Office de Tourisme.

"We'll stop at spots you recognize from his paintings. Then I'll guide you back to 1890, and we'll see what you pick up."

She nodded. "That should work if the undiscovered paintings are scenes he painted multiple times. Otherwise, the one copy of the painting has already been found."

He groaned. "I hadn't thought of that." He ran his hand through his hair. "We'll have to cover the whole town."

"Perhaps not. Vincent often repainted the same scene. For example..." Stopping, she looked back along the street. She laughed and clapped her hands, pointing up the hill they had just descended.

"There," she said. "'Village Street and Steps in Auvers with Two Figures.' I can still recognize the scene even today."

Two figures, he thought. *Laure and I.*

Three. I'm still here.

"But," she said, "he painted it again—with five figures and different lighting and colors. Same scene, two separate paintings. Why not three?"

He nodded. "So this might work." They set out again.

Auvers was a small town and unchanged in many ways from the time when van Gogh had lived there. Signs and arrows everywhere marked anything related to the painter. Laure was continually delighted as they walked the narrow, well-marked streets. It seemed that wherever they turned, she could point out a scene captured in a painting by the man known in that town simply as Vincent.

They came to a small inn. The sign overhead read "L'Auberge Ravoux." Laure stopped. "This was owned by Arthur Gustave Ravoux. Vincent lived here. His bedroom is upstairs. The town has kept it intact."

"Perfect. Let's go up," he said, heading for the door.

"No," Laure said, stepping back. "I've seen pictures of it. Grey-blue closets, bare wooden floor, white plastered walls, high window in a peaked ceiling."

"But wouldn't where he lived be a good place for viewing?"

She shook her head. "He didn't paint there." She looked across the street to a small café. "We've been walking all morning. Why don't we have lunch?"

There's something more here, Elise said.

She's tired. She's hungry.

She's afraid. She's broken.

They went into the café. Laure ordered a noisette and a croissant, Maroch an espresso and ham on a baguette.

"Where should we start then," he asked as they ate, "if not his room?"

She glanced across at the Auberge again, then looked away. "For viewing?" She sipped her coffee. "L'église. The church."

How sweet. Where you first kissed her.

"He painted there," she continued. "And it is peaceful, quiet. I will need that."

He paid their bill. As they left the café, Laure looked at the Auberge again. "He painted their daughter, Adeline. I wonder if she went upstairs for the sitting, to his room…"

"I thought you said he didn't paint there."

She turned away from the inn, as if she hadn't heard him. "I want to go to the church."

Broken, my love.

In the churchyard, Laure once again found the angle from which Vincent had painted the scene. She settled onto the grass facing the church.

He sat beside her. "What type of viewer are you? Visual? Auditory? Touch? I need to know if I'm to guide you."

"Visual, mostly," she said. "Probably because I'm a painter."

He nodded. "There's often a correlation to a creative skill. I knew a chef who always picked up smells first."

"But I also pick up on people, especially if they are displaying strong emotions."

He remembered Karsh's story of her finding the Russian general. "Let's focus on the visual to start. Ready?"

She nodded, sitting cross-legged in lotus position, hands on her knees, eyes open and focused on the church.

"I want you to visualize the inside of the church," he began, his voice low.

Laure's expression went blank as she seemed to stare at something just beyond the stone walls. "I see it," she whispered. "But there are multiple images, overlapping each other…"

"You're picking up scenes from different periods in time. We'll sort through those. Now step back ten years."

Pause. "They've changed the carpet. It's blue. And the organ is different, smaller."

"Good. Now I want you to stay in that time, but pull back to the outside of the church, the same view you are facing now."

"The stone is dirtier. They must have cleaned it since."

"Good. Stay outside. Now step back another ten years."

They continued in that way, with Maroch slowly guiding Laure back through time. He made notes as they went, so that Karsh could later verify Laure's observations against the church's archives.

They reached 1900. "Laure," he said, "move back to 1890 now, when Vincent arrived in Auvers. Tell me what you see."

She shivered. "It's quite cool. There are no wild flowers in the grass, and the trees are bare, so we're earlier than when he painted it." She paused. "It feels like March."

He checked his notes. Vincent had painted the church in June. Maroch didn't know which day, and he wasn't sure that he could direct Laure to a specific date anyway.

"I want you to go forward in time a bit. To June."

She nodded, and then smiled. "It's warm. The sun is shining. I see the flowers from the painting now. People are walking past the church. Someone is nearby." She stopped. After a moment, Laure started mouthing words under her breath. She would pause occasionally and nod or smile, as if in conversation with some unseen person.

She also picks up on people…

…especially if they're displaying strong emotions.

"Laure?" No reply. "Laure? Can you still hear me?" Still no reply. He waited. Finally, concerned that she had slipped into a trance state, he gently shook her shoulder.

She looked around, seemingly dazed.

"Are you all right?" he asked.

This girl is far from all right.

She stared at him with a blank expression.

"Laure, who were you talking with?"

You know.

She gazed at the church. "Beautiful," she whispered.

"Laure!"

She looked back at him, as if she'd forgotten he was there. "I need to go to Paris. To the Musée d'Orsay. I need to see his works. The real ones."

"Laure! *Who* were you talking to?"

You know.

She stared at him with that same unfocused look.

"Vincent," she said.

❧

Maroch moves on to the next painting. In "Undergrowth with two figures—June, 1890," a man and a woman stand in a wood, their faces obscured. The foreground lies in bright sunshine, the trees growing in neat, straight lines. But in the far background, the trees creep together into a dark jungle that no sunlight penetrates.

The couple stands in the undergrowth between the sunlight ahead and the shadows at their backs. The man faces the viewer, as if intent on leaving the woods. But the woman stares over her shoulder at the darkness behind.

What did you think? That you would lead her out of those woods? Bring her into the light?

She was my light, Elise. My way out. We were in the same woods, on the same path.

Every path has two directions, my love.

The Musée d'Orsay was closed by the time they drove in to Paris, but Maroch had called ahead. The Director met them and led them to the van Gogh gallery. She left them alone, except for a single guard watching discreetly from a doorway.

Laure stared at Vincent's "L'Église d'Auvers." She had barely said a word during the drive, finally falling asleep.

"I saw him beginning to paint this," she said, raising a hand towards the painting.

The guard stepped forward immediately, but Maroch stopped Laure before she could touch it. *It's as if part of her is still there.*

This girl was never all here to start with.

"Laure—"

"He is..." She looked at Maroch, blinking. "...was... so lonely. He likes...liked people, enjoyed people. He just didn't know how to love in a way they could understand."

"You actually talked to Vincent?" he said, unwilling to believe.

"He works so fast. He was frightened at first, when I spoke to him, in his mind. He thought he was possessed. But I told him that his painting was beautiful. That his work was important." She looked back to the painting of the church. "We talked about painting. He called me his Angel."

"Laure, I've never experienced that before—contacting someone during viewing. Have you?"

"I have sensed minds, but never communicated with them. And never into the past."

"How do you explain it?"

She shrugged. "I don't. I can't even explain how I can view." She looked around the gallery, at Vincent's paintings surrounding them. "But he was in such pain. He was crying out every day. Perhaps I just heard his cry." She stared at the church again. "He is still crying out, through his paintings." She shook her head. "So much pain."

He stared at her. *Pain and beauty.*

And that worked out so well for Vincent…

They returned to the cottage. Over the next week, Maroch was able to guide Laure into contact with Vincent at other locations in Auvers. By the second week, she could establish a link just as easily at the cottage, so they stopped the trips into town to provide her more viewing time. Her favorite viewing position was on the floor in the sitting room in front of the bouquet of flowers she had made from the garden, with one of the books open to a painting by Vincent to use as her focusing point.

Maroch began to worry about Laure's mental state. The more time she spent with Vincent, the more withdrawn she became. They still made love, but he had greater and greater difficulty in engaging her in conversation about anything beyond Vincent.

There is pain in beauty, my love. And there is much pain in this beauty.

Karsh visited the second week. He and Maroch drove in to Auvers, partly so they would not disturb Laure, but mostly so they would not be overheard. They sat on the patio of the café across from the Auberge Ravoux.

Karsh was skeptical. "How do we know she's not imagining this contact?"

"You said her observations from these viewings all check out."

Karsh shrugged. "She knows as much about Vincent as any scholar. She could just be channeling that knowledge. Besides, who gives a shit? I don't. We're looking for paintings…"

I don't care about the paintings anymore, Maroch thought.

But you care about her.

"…and she's come up with squat on that front," Karsh finished, shaking his head. "I don't like depending on someone who hears voices in their head."

And what's wrong with hearing voices? Elise asked.

Maroch reddened. "She's with him each day. She sees every painting he works on. If he does one that hasn't been discovered, we'll know about it. Then I can use that painting to refocus her viewing and locate it."

Karsh snorted. "Assuming you can get her to refocus, to leave her precious tragic artist." He sighed. "But you're right. Assuming she's not making all this up, this can still pay off."

Maroch looked across the street to where Vincent had lived. "That depends on what she finds."

No, my love. It depends on what she's really looking for.

In the gallery, Maroch stares at Vincent's next painting. His hand begins to tremble.

A path snakes through a wheat field that bends under the wind. A blue-black sky foreshadows a coming storm. A flock of crows rises from the wheat into that dark sky, fading into small black ghosts in the distance.

He reads the plaque.

> "*Crows over a Wheat Field* (Auvers, July, 1890): One of van Gogh's final paintings, some view the crows as a presage of death and interpret its ominous tone and meandering paths as a 'suicide note' (van Gogh shot himself shortly after this work was completed)."

He covers his face as his tears come and his body shakes with his sobs. *She didn't even leave me a note.*

She was *the note,* Elise says gently. *You just couldn't read her.*

In late July, Karsh dropped by the cottage for his weekly visit. He greeted Maroch, then turned to where Laure sat staring unfocused at the bouquet of flowers, her lips occasionally moving in silence.

"She looks like shit," Karsh said.

He was right. Laure's face was pale and drawn, and she'd lost weight. Maroch swallowed. "I've tried to get her to cut back her viewing time, get more rest, eat more." He shook his head. "She says that she's getting close, that she's afraid she'll miss something important."

Karsh snorted. "Let us hope she finds something before she kills herself trying, my friend." He nodded at the bouquet. "Those flowers are standing up better than she is." He walked out to the car.

Maroch looked at the bouquet. The flowers seemed as fresh as when Laure had first picked them weeks ago. He shrugged. What did he know about flowers?

As much as you know about this girl.

They drove into Auvers and sat on the patio at the same café across from the Auberge Ravoux. The day was warm and sunny, the opposite of Maroch's mood. They ordered espressos, and Karsh lit a cigarette. "I rented you a place in St. Remy for August. Maybe you'll have better luck there."

"I think we should take a break. Let Laure rest. Get her strength back," Maroch said. "I'm worried about her."

Karsh studied him with narrowed eyes for a moment. Then he gave a big grin around yellow teeth. "Jesus, you're fucking her, aren't you?"

Maroch's face got hot. Karsh laughed. "I thought you would have learned after Elise—" He broke off suddenly. Maroch's hand had flashed out, his fingertips closing on Karsh's throat. "Christ..." Karsh croaked as Maroch's grip tightened. A couple at a nearby table looked over at them then quickly turned away.

"There are lines, Karsh," Maroch rasped through clenched teeth, "that you do not cross." He let go and sat back in his chair again.

Karsh gasped in a breath. Rubbing his throat, he glared at Maroch. He took a drag and coughed it out. "Fuck you. Do what you want with her. Just find me some paintings." He looked away. "You're as crazy as she is," he muttered.

There's something here, my love.

"What do you mean?" Maroch asked.

Karsh smirked at him.

Ask him.

"Tell me, Karsh," he asked again, steel in his voice.

Karsh considered him then shrugged. "The Company learned something early on: that the best viewers are people with a traumatic episode in their past. That's why they moved you into the program after you were almost killed."

She's broken, my love.

Maroch's gut tightened. "What does that have to do with Laure?"

Karsh took another drag and let out the smoke. "The Company found her in a psycho hospital in Montreal. She tested off the scale as a viewer, so they used their Canadian contacts to get her released—and get the charges dropped."

Maroch's hand was trembling again. He moved it to his lap. "What charges?" he asked, fighting a quaver in his voice.

"Murder. Shot a man. Got off on an insanity plea."

Broken.

Maroch looked across to the Auberge, remembering Laure's words: *I wonder if she went upstairs. To his room.*

"It was her father, wasn't it?" he whispered.

Karsh nodded.

Maroch shook his head. "She said…she told me that they were close."

Karsh snorted. "Closer than they should have been. Ever since she was a kid." He laughed. "You should have seen the paintings she did during the Russian project. She was pretty fucked up. Probably still is." He looked at Maroch. "Surprised she let you touch her, let alone bone her. She must really trust you." He rubbed his throat. "Fuck if I know why."

Maroch felt something slipping away inside him. "Victims like her, they often sexualize their adult relationships," Maroch whispered, his voice sounding as if it was coming from someone else. *Everything she told me was a lie.*

No, Elise whispered. *She loves you. And I understand why.*

He looked at Karsh. "If her father didn't commit suicide, why her obsession with van Gogh?"

Karsh shrugged. "Her father *was* a painter. Her shrinks said she's convinced herself that he really did commit suicide, that she developed her obsession to reinforce her delusion. What the fuck do I know? Or care? As long as she finds something."

They drove back in silence, the countryside of Vincent's paintings flashing by, Maroch seeing nothing but Laure's face in each scene. Karsh pulled up at the cottage, and Maroch got out.

"I'll pick you up next week," Karsh said, "to take you both to St. Remy." He started to pull away, then stopped and leaned out the window. "You said something earlier —about Laure being afraid of 'missing something' when she isn't viewing."

Maroch nodded. "Something in Vincent's life that day."

"Why couldn't she pick it up later?"

"This link she has with him—it isn't like normal viewing. She doesn't get flashes of random images. Somehow, she's moving along in real time with him, day by day. An hour of viewing is an hour in Vincent's life, same day as we're in now, except the year is 1890. If she misses a day, it's gone."

Karsh checked the date on his watch. "Well, she'll be taking a break soon, whether she wants to or not."

"What do you mean?"

"Van Gogh killed himself in July 1890. Can't remember the day, but we're running out of July—it's already the twenty-seventh." Shifting the van into gear, Karsh drove away.

Alone in front of the cottage, Maroch watched the van disappear. Despite the warm sun, a chill was crawling up his spine.

July twenty-seventh, he thought.

Do you remember that date?

He spun around. His Citroën was missing.

"Laure!" he shouted. He ran into the cottage, calling her name. She wasn't in the sitting room. Upstairs, both bedrooms were empty.

Laure was gone. He checked the drawer in the table beside his bed where he kept his gun, a Russian Glock. The gun was missing too.

Downstairs, he slumped into one of the worn armchairs. The vase with the bouquet stood undisturbed on the low table, the flowers still alive, but for the first time, beginning to wilt. Beside the vase, a book lay open to a painting: "Crows over a Wheat Field, Auvers, July 1890."

Phrases in the accompanying text seemed to rise from the page to stand out in relief against the other words, pulling his eyes to them.

One of his final paintings…presage of death…suicide note…

Across the top of the page, Laure had scrawled something.

Je suis dans une humeur de calme presque trop grande…la tristesse finit aujourd'hui.

He mouthed the words under his breath. "'I am in a mood of nearly too great calmness…the sadness ends today.'"

He remembered Laure's words when they had first walked into Auvers. *'I am in a mood of nearly too great calmness…' He wrote that on July 27, 1890. Later that day…Later that day…*

…he shot himself.

Maroch stood up. *Today is the twenty-seventh.*

Where are you going?

I have to find her.

How? Where will you look?

Auvers…or the Musée…or… He dropped into the chair again. *I don't know.* He buried his head in his hands. *How can I find her?*

You know how, my love.

His hands began to shake. *I can't. I haven't since you…*

You must. You are her only hope.

No.

She trusted you.

He stared at the wilting bouquet in front of him, remembering the day Laure had made it, the day they had first kissed, first made love. His hands balled into fists. *I'll try.*

I know.

Focusing on the vase of flowers, the nearest thing that spoke to him of Laure, he cleared his mind of all images but the bouquet and her face. Slowly, the old familiar sensation of floating returned, of being suspended in another place even while knowing that he still sat in the cottage staring at the bouquet.

Staring at the bouquet...

Staring...

The bouquet suddenly changed, becoming brighter and more alive, yet at the same time more blurred and more... abstract.

It's a painting, he thought.

It's his *painting.*

"It's so beautiful."

The voice sounded in his head, but it was not his voice, and it was not Elise. He swallowed. "Laure," he whispered.

"I am here, my love," Laure answered. "Can you see it? It's hanging in the Musée. It wasn't here before. It's our bouquet. He painted it from my mind. He painted it for me."

"Laure..."

"He's dying. I was with him when he shot himself. He couldn't love in a way they understood. So much pain. So much beauty. I couldn't stop him. I couldn't make him stop. I wanted him to stop."

The image of the painting disappeared as Laure looked down, and he saw what she held in her hand. A gun. Maroch's gun.

"He used to say he painted for me. So much beauty. So much pain. I couldn't make him stop."

She doesn't mean Vincent.

"Laure," he whispered to her, "put down the gun."

"He didn't know how to love me in a way I could understand. I couldn't make him stop."

The painting of the bouquet floated before her eyes again, superimposed for Maroch with the real bouquet in front of him.

"He called me his Angel," Laure said softly.

He felt her arm move. He tasted the cold metal of the gun barrel in her mouth.

"Laure!" he screamed out loud, leaping to his feet. "No!"

A blade of pain ripped his skull open. His head snapped back. The image of the painting exploded into searing light. His legs collapsed, and he slumped to the floor, cracking his head against the table.

He huddled there, weeping, until the sobs that wracked his body finally stopped. "Laure?" he whispered, reaching for her, calling for her with his mind.

Silence.

I'm sorry, my love, Elise said softly.

He opened his eyes. In front of him stood the bouquet. As he lay there, unable to move, a faded petal slipped from the single red rose and fell to the table.

Completing his circuit of the gallery, Maroch stands again before the final painting, the one beneath which Laure had taken her life, where her blood now stains the plush carpet.

The flowers are mostly white and yellow chrysanthemums, pale colors mixing with the green of the leaves and stems.

A pale bouquet, like her.

And a fragile one.

Two chrysanthemums sit at the top right of the bouquet, their petals mostly white, but tinged with red at the edges, as if they are blushing at their tips. The flowers stand beside each other in the vase, close but not touching. To the left, another pair of flowers, all red, nestle against each other. Finally, his eyes come to rest on the single, large, red rose in the center of the bouquet near the bottom.

He remembers Laure's words. *Two hearts, one rhythm. Two souls, one journey.*

Your heart still beats, my love, whispers Elise. *Your journey is not yet over.*

The Director comes to stand beside him. "Strange," she mutters, more to the picture than to him.

It was there.

"I checked our records," she says. "This painting *is* there. We acquired it from a private collector in ninety-five. Strange…" She bites her lip, then shrugs. "Do you need me anymore?" she asks. "I need to attend to…matters." She glances at the bloodstained carpet.

He shakes his head. She leaves him.

For a few minutes longer, he stands staring at the painting. He checks his watch. Five o'clock. *One more thing to do.*

He turns to the door, but stops. Kneeling, he brushes his fingertips over where Laure had lain, touching her blood, stroking the carpet the way he had once caressed her naked skin. He begins to weep, his tears flowing, his breath coming in great sobs. Finally, he stands again. With one last look at the painting, he leaves the Musée.

Karsh's black van is outside the cottage. Maroch parks the Citroën behind it, blocking it in.

The vase with the bouquet still sits on the low table, the flowers now corpses of their former beauty. Karsh is in the kitchen, throwing fat file folders of Maroch's notes into boxes. He looks up as Maroch enters. The sharp features of his face crease into a broad grin. He points to a book on the table, open to Vincent's painting of the bouquet, a painting that did not exist a day ago.

"Maroch, my friend! Did you *see* the painting? Yes, of course! You told me! My god! What we have done! Nothing will be the same after this."

"I know," Maroch replies quietly. *Only too well.*

Karsh laughs like a gleeful child on Christmas morning. "You know. I know. But no one else." He tosses another file into the nearest box. "I figured it out. *We* must be aware of the change because we are so close to its source. You know, so close to Laure."

So close. No more.

Maroch reaches inside his jacket. His Glock, retrieved from the cleanup team at the Musée, feels cold and heavy in his hand. *Like my heart.* He points it at Karsh.

Karsh stares stupidly at the gun, his normal air of animal cunning gone. "Maroch? What…" His eyes dart from the gun to Maroch's face. He swallows. "Fifty per cent. Equal partners."

Maroch shakes his head slowly.

"More?" Karsh snaps, but the smile returns quickly. "Fine. Yes, fine. What do you want?"

"The things I want," Maroch says, his voice a dead thing, "you can't give me."

Karsh's mouth opens and closes several times before any words come out, the fear now naked in his wide eyes. "Maroch, for God's sake. We changed the past!"

"And you'll try to do it again," Maroch says quietly.

Karsh shakes his head so hard Maroch can hear vertebrae crack. He raises his hands in an entreaty before him. They are trembling so much they seem to blur. "No! I swear."

"Someone will. The Company. Someone. With knowledge you'll sell them."

"But this—this is *power*," Karsh snarls, disbelief momentarily overcoming his fear. "Real power. Power like no one has ever held."

"That no one should hold."

"But, Maroch, my God—"

"She's dead," Maroch says, his own voice a stranger to his ears, as if someone else is speaking, someone who believes the words.

Karsh blinks. "What? Dead? How?" He looks at the gun, then at Maroch.

"Not me. She killed herself."

Sweat glistens on Karsh's face now. "Then it's over. She was the key. There's no need…" He stares at the gun.

Maroch shakes his head. "You know it can be done. You'll try again."

The cunning finally returns to Karsh's face, like a fox peeking from the underbrush. "Yes. Yes! It *can* be done. The past can be changed. Think what that means! Are there not things in your life that you would change?"

You know what he means, my love, Elise whispers.

Maroch's eyes slip from Karsh's face. His hand on the Glock wavers, but then steadies.

It's too late. She had the power.

You have power, too.

"What did you think of it?" Maroch asks, his voice almost wistful.

Pulling his eyes from the gun, Karsh looks at him, confusion mixing with fear on his face. "What?"

"The painting. What did you think of the painting?"

Karsh stares at him as if he's crazy. "My God, Maroch," he sobs. "It's a fucking painting. What does that matter?"

Maroch shoots Karsh through the heart. Karsh stumbles backwards and crashes to the floor. Maroch fires a bullet into his forehead and another into his chest.

The blood spreads out from Karsh's body onto the wooden floor, like Laure's blood, like the single, lonely, red rose in the painting.

"I thought," Maroch whispers, "that it was beautiful."

In the bedroom upstairs, he can still smell Laure. He picks up a pillow and presses it to his face, the cotton cool on his fevered skin. He breathes her in, her smell, his memories of their love-making. Sinking onto the bed, he weeps, his tears soaking the pillow, washing away her smell but not his pain. He throws the pillow to the floor and goes downstairs.

In the sitting room, he slumps against the table with the vase, shaking loose a few more brittle petals. A book on Vincent lies open on the floor. He stares at the painting then reads the text.

> "*Half-Figure of an Angel*: Based on 'The Angel Raphael' by Rembrandt. Raphael is the guardian angel of humanity, protector of the young and innocent. The face of this Angel is full of sorrow…"

He remembers seeing this painting when they first moved into the cottage. That angel had long red hair, heavy features, and a broad nose. He stares at the painting. *This* angel has short hair, black and shiny, framing a round, pale face. Small rosebud mouth, short delicate nose, large green eyes.

Laure.

He called her his Angel.

Protector of the young and innocent. But who was to protect her?

I was.

You could never have saved her. She was too full of sorrow.

He reaches into his pocket. He takes out the Glock again.

No! Elise screams in his mind.

The sadness will never end… He puts the barrel of the gun in his mouth.

No! It can end, my love. She gave you the key. Karsh gave you the key. You can change the past. Are there not things in your past that you would change?

He hesitates, his finger on the trigger. *That power died with her.*

Liar. You know it can be done. That's why you killed Karsh.

I don't have her power, he replies, but he lowers the gun.

You have your own. Vincent repainted scenes. Why not you?

He stares at the bouquet. *Together again? Could it be possible?* He puts the Glock on the floor and pushes it away.

Which one of us do you mean? Elise asks.

Why must I choose? But then his heart sinks as the realization hits him. If he saves Laure from her childhood, she will never go into the hospital. Karsh will never find her. Maroch will never meet her, never have this one chance to save Elise.

If he saves Elise, Karsh will never recruit him for this project. He will never meet Laure, never have this opportunity to save her from her father.

His resolve wavers. How can he choose between the two women he has loved?

Unless…

Which one of us do you mean? Elise asks again.

He begins to focus on the flowers, clearing his mind of the room around him, of his pain. The old feeling returns, as if he is floating…

Which one, my love?

⚘

The little girl lay awake in her bed. She could hear her father moving in the kitchen downstairs. Soon, she knew, he would come up. He would come into her room.

He would call her his Angel.

She pulled the covers over her head, curling herself up as small as she could, trying to disappear. Maybe he wouldn't visit her tonight. Maybe…

Laure!

The girl sat up. There was a voice in her head. At first, she was frightened. But her fear disappeared. The voice reminded her of how her mother used to talk to her.

"Oui?" she answered. The voice spoke to her, telling her what she must do. She listened, then quietly got out of bed. In the hall outside her room, she carefully lifted the phone from the small table and dialed the number of an aunt who lived nearby. The aunt answered, and the child began to talk. She was crying by the end. But it was done. It was finally said.

Slipping back into her room, she went to her desk. The voice told her of one more thing that she must do. As she wrote the letter about a woman named Elise and addressed the envelope to a man named Maroch, she wondered who the voice was.

By the time she finished, she had decided that it was an angel.

In the old part of Montreal, Maroch and Elise stroll hand in hand through a small art gallery. A group of visitors stands before a painting, listening to a pretty young brunette.

"I saw you," Elise says, with a mischievous smile.

"What?" Maroch replies.

"Checking her out. That young artist."

He smiles. "This is her exhibit. I was admiring her work."

"I saw what you were admiring. And on our second honeymoon, too." She kisses him. "But I forgive you. She *is* beautiful."

He looks at the girl again. Short hair, black and shiny, framing a round, pale face. Small rosebud mouth, short delicate nose, large green eyes. "Yes," he says softly. "She is."

Elise considers the girl's paintings. "Talented too. Reminds me of van Gogh—but without the pain." She nudges him. "Want to go chat her up?"

He pulls Elise close and kisses her. "One beauty in my life is enough. Besides," he says, watching the artist laughing and talking, "she seems happy enough without me."

As they are leaving the gallery, he stops. "I want to sign her guest book."

Elise nods and smiles. "I'll see you outside."

He waits until she has left before removing an envelope from his jacket pocket. It is creased and dog-eared, and the ink is beginning to fade. It is addressed to him. He stares at the name on the return address.

Laure Armand.

He looks across the room at the young artist with the same name. He thinks again of approaching her, of asking her. Asking her how she had known, how she possibly could have known to warn them of that night in Lisbon.

He decides—again—that he doesn't want to know. Instead, he turns the envelope over and on the back, he writes in French, 'To our angel. Thank you.' He tucks it into the guest book, and, with one last look at Laure, he follows Elise out into the warm July sun.

STORY NOTES

Early in this story, Maroch reads a plaque beside the impossible and beautiful painting of the story title:

> "This still life is not mentioned in van Gogh's letters and has puzzled scholars as to its place in his artistic production. Most certainly a late work and possibly the Museum's first painting from his Auvers period (May-July1890)."

That is taken from the actual plaque for the actual painting, "Bouquet of Flowers in a Vase" by the Dutch artist, Vincent van Gogh. The painting hangs (usually), not in the Musée d'Orsay in Paris, but rather in the Metropolitan Museum of Art in New York City. In art books, the painting is sometimes titled "Chrysanthemums and Wild Flowers in Vase", but "chrysanthemums" is too hard to pronounce for a story title.

Art is a passion of mine. When I travel, I try to visit the local art museums in that city, with a special interest in European art from the mid-1800's through the surrealists. But my favorite artist has long been Vincent. I've seen (I think) every publicly viewable painting of his in every museum in every city I've ever visited. I've read his letters with his brother, Theo, and ever so many biographies.

I also love writing stories about other creative artistic pursuits, whether they involve music ("Symphony"), sculpture

("Enlightenment"), or dance ("The Dancer at the Red Door"), as well as at least one other story about an artist ("By Her Hand, She Draws You Down"). But I'd always especially wanted to write a story about Vincent. I'd tried to write that story many years ago. Not this version, but still a story about a woman in our time in love with Vincent and who (somehow) actually managed to meet him. The "somehow's" that I tried didn't work for me, so that story stayed in my head.

But that yet-to-be-told (or even defined) story about Vincent stayed with me, tickling me every now and then to remind me that it was still waiting to be born, until one day found me in front of "Bouquet of Flowers in a Vase" in the MMoA. I'd never seen the painting before, which was cool enough, but when I read the plaque, I knew that I had to use this somehow in my Vincent story. Van Gogh is one of the most researched artists of all time, and because of his extensive letter correspondence with his beloved brother, Theo, we have a running commentary of his entire artistic career, including what paintings he was working on at any time. For a painting to be unmentioned and undated was a wonderful mystery.

But I still didn't have my time travel "somehow". Then one evening, a writer friend was discussing remote viewing and how it had been used in the field of one of her passions, archeology, to search for the lost tomb of Alexander the Great.

Somewhere in that conversation, the penny dropped, and I knew I had my time travel "somehow" to link my heroine in modern time to Vincent in the past. I did some research on remote viewing, from which came my former CIA operative, Maroch, added some tragedy in his past and a search for lost paintings, and the story started to take shape.

I hope that you enjoyed it.

Spirit Dance

In the beginning of things, men were as animals and animals as men.

—Cree legend

Vera made a warding sign as I entered the store, my hound Gelert trailing behind me. She pretended to wipe her hands on her faded blue apron, but I caught the dance of her fingers.

"Hello, Vera. It's been a while," I said.

"Yes, yes it has, Mr. Blaidd," she said too quickly, not returning my smile. Turning from where she'd been refilling a food bin, she addressed her husband. "I gotta check something in the back, Ed." Almost running, she slipped behind the long wooden counter and into the storeroom at the rear of the store.

Edward Two Rivers leaned on the counter beside the cash register, a newspaper spread in front of him, his long gray hair spilling onto the pages. He watched her leave then smiled at me.

"Ouch," I said.

"You still spook her," he chuckled.

"Are you going to run and hide too?" I asked, grinning.

The black eyes narrowed, but his smile remained. "Vera's a white woman. My people have told legends of the Heroka for generations, Grey Legs. I grew up with those stories. I've known others of your kind…and I think I still know you, even if it's been…what?"

"Four years," I said.

"Four years since you left Wawa." He took my offered hand in a strong grip.

"Good to see you, Ed," I said.

"You too, Gwyn." Leaning over the counter, he patted Gelert's huge head. "And good to see you as well, you great beast." Gelert's tail wagged furiously, threatening a display of pop cans. Ed looked back to me. "Did you fly in?"

I nodded. "I landed on Deer's Pond, set up camp on the north shore, then we hiked in. Get my email?"

"Yeah. I made you up some supplies and a map to the truck driver's cabin." He nodded toward a small pile of brown paper packages in the corner, wrapped in twine.

"Thanks. What do I owe you?"

"I'll run a tab. You'll be here a while. Not the best home-coming for you, I guess."

"Could be better. Any word of Robert?"

Ed nodded. "I showed your friend's picture around. He was definitely here in Wawa for the funerals, but kept to himself pretty much. Found someone who talked to him, though. She said he left town about two days ago, but he'd be back. Something about unfinished business here."

"Any idea where he went?"

"Just a guess, but I'd say the Muskokas."

"Why?" I asked, puzzled. The Muskokas were a cottage and resort district a two-hour drive north of Toronto, and a good seven hundred kilometers from Wawa.

He held up a finger for an answer and started flipping through the newspaper. Gelert curled beside our supplies. I waited, sifting through the smells of grains and fruit, wood and burlap—and humans. Vera was muttering in the storeroom at the back. I could have made out her words if I had wanted to, but I didn't.

Ed began reading. "'Local logging baron Jonathan Conrad and his bodyguard were found dead early yesterday morning, outside his lodge in the Muskokas.'"

Footsteps outside announced a customer to me before the bell over the door brought Ed's head up from the paper. She looked early twenties, tall and slim with gray green eyes and long dark hair that wasn't sure where it wanted to rest. Flashing a quick smile at Ed, she moved to the shelves of canned goods.

"Morning, Leiddia," Ed said, eyebrows shooting up.

"Morning, Ed," she replied, then looked at me. A familiar aura tinged her outline. She kept looking as I turned back to Ed.

Ed continued reading, his voice lower. "It says Conrad's wife had gone into town for the evening. She found the bodies about two yesterday morning."

"How'd he die?" I asked.

The woman Ed called Leiddia turned toward Ed, but I could feel her eyes still on me. I didn't look at her.

"They're bringing the coroner up from Toronto. The cops figure some kind of animal attack, judging from the wounds. They say it was big whatever it was." Ed looked up at me. "Maybe a bear."

I swore silently at that last bit of news. "Guess the environmentalists won't grieve much."

"The parents of those three boys won't," Leiddia said, stepping closer to the counter. "He killed them, even if he didn't drive the truck. Everybody knows he gave the order."

"Got off though," sighed Ed. "So'd the truck driver. Accident, they said. Bad brakes. Conrad got a five-hundred dollar fine for not maintaining his trucks."

I had heard about the truck incident three days ago. Conrad had been chairman for a company that owned the paper mill outside Wawa and several logging operations north of Lake Superior. Recently, the company had faced escalating pressure from local residents, native bands, and environmental groups. Protests centered on the company's clear cutting methods and general contempt for the old growth forest. The confrontation climaxed when a group of students and other protesters blockaded the road leading to the current clear cutting target.

The first truck to reach the blockade had backed off, driving fifteen miles back to camp in reverse. Two hours later, the next truck arrived. This one hadn't stopped.

The kids hadn't used logs or fallen trees to block the road. They hadn't piled boulders, or sprinkled the road with tire punctures. They had just stood across it, arms linked, singing.

The truck slammed into them, killing three local students. A female protestor from out-of-town also died.

"Five hundred dollars," said Ed, shaking his head.

"I went to college with one of them," Leiddia said quietly.

I looked at her, confirming my first impression of the familiar aura. "Were you there?"

She shook her head. "My stepfather works in the mill. He wouldn't let me go." She stared at me hard.

Ed cleared his throat. "Uh, Grey Legs, this is Leiddia Barker. Leiddia, this is an old friend, Gwyn Blaidd. Gwyn's the friend of Mr. Arcas I mentioned."

"You know Robert?" she asked.

The door to the store opened before I could reply. A man stood with one foot in the store, hand still on the door. "Leiddia!" he barked, "Hurry up!"

She didn't look at him. "I'm coming," she snapped, thumping some cans on the counter.

As Ed rang up the order, I looked the man over. Late forties, maybe six feet, a paunch and thinning black hair slicked back. Gelert growled at him, and I didn't stop him. I didn't like his smell.

Leiddia paid Ed, took the bag of groceries, and turned to the door. Not waiting for her, the man let the door slam, walked to a beat-up Cutlass parked in front and got in. He had never even looked my way. As Leiddia shifted the bag to her other arm, I stepped past her and opened the door.

"Thanks," she said, stepping through. Hesitating, she looked at the car, then back at me. "Blaidd. That's a strange name."

"It's Welsh."

"Why does Ed call you Grey Legs?"

The car's horn blared. Jumping out of the car, he moved quickly toward us, fists clenched. "Damn it! What're you doing?" he snarled at her, then spun to face me. "Who the hell are you, mister? I…" His voice trailed off.

"Hello, Tom," I said. "Long time."

He swallowed hard. "Gwyn! I didn't know you were back."

I smiled. "I didn't figure our past relationship called for a postcard."

"Uh, yeah. Uh, Leiddia, don't be too long. I gotta get to work." He turned and got back in the Olds, with a glance over his shoulder.

She raised an eyebrow, staring after him. "Never seen anything affect old Tommy like that." She looked me up and down. "Will I see you again?"

"I'm camping by Deer's Pond. North shore," I said.

Smiling a cat-with-the-canary smile, she strolled casually to the car and got in. They drove off, and I went back inside.

"So what do you think of our Leiddia?" Ed asked.

"I think I just passed some kind of test. She's the one who talked to Robert?"

"Yeah. I said an old friend of his was coming into town and wanted to surprise him. That's when she told me about him leaving." He looked puzzled. "Weird her showing up just as you arrive. She's not in town much. You gonna go see her?"

"I'm guessing she'll find me. How does Tom Barker come to be her stepfather?"

Ed grimaced. "She and her mom moved here about two years ago. The mother had some money and a good property, which got Tom interested. Don't know what she saw in him."

"He's still the same?"

"Grade-A asshole? Yeah, plus there's been some incidents with him and her mother. Cops at the house, but she's never laid any charges."

"Physical abuse?"

He nodded. "Vera knows the night nurse at Mercy. The mother's been in a few times, always with a story about some accident around the home. The nurse said it looked more like beatings." Ed looked grim, then thoughtful. "Far as I know, he leaves the girl alone."

"From what I saw," I said, picking up my supplies and moving to the door, "pushing Leiddia too far would be very inadvisable. He might wake something."

Ed's eyes narrowed. "What'd you see in her?"

"She has the Mark," I said quietly. Opening the door, I stepped out into the street after Gelert, not waiting for Ed's reply.

The first frost had come to Wawa early. Gelert and I hiked back through fall colors, crisp air, and no mosquitoes, reaching our campsite overlooking Deer's Pond just before sunset.

That night, spirits of the firelight danced around me through the trees as the rising moon silvered the smooth surface of the water. With Gelert snoring softly beside me, other spirits danced through my thoughts.

I didn't want them to dance. I didn't want them to even exist. But spirits have their own views on these matters, and are very persistent when they feel it's time for a performance. These ghosts went back fifteen years. The prompting for tonight's tango was much more recent.

Dance, spirits.

Three days before, I had been many miles north. That day, I had stood by the heavy wooden railing of the broad stone promenade running the length of Cil y Blaidd, watching a small seaplane shatter the glass of the lake below. Part carved, part hung from a rocky slope of forest, Cil y Blaidd is a sprawling wood and stone structure overlooking a lake in far northern Ontario. The name is Welsh, for Wolf's Lair.

Built to my design years ago as an occasional retreat from civilization, recently it had become my permanent home. Or perhaps it was my act of retreat that had become permanent.

Accessible only by seaplane, Cil y Blaidd is invisible from the air. Those who had built it had been flown in at night, stayed until completion, and then were flown out again at night. I had piloted the plane.

Only three other people knew its location. As I watched the plane taxi to shore, I wondered which of the three it carried.

The plane pulled up to a long dock hidden from above by arching willow branches. A huge male figure emerged and strode along the dock to stone steps carved from the cliff face.

Well, it's not Estelle, I thought, ignoring the resentment this brought even after fifteen years. Too far to see if it was Robert or Michel. My visitor looked up, searching the slope as he climbed. Our eyes met, and he raised a meaty hand to remove and wave a cloth cap, revealing a mass of red curls.

"Lo, Mitch," I called down as I waved back, wondering briefly at my feeling of relief. Turning from the railing, I headed through the house to greet Michel Ducharmes, the Red Bull, and current head of the Circle of the Heroka.

Opening huge oaken front doors, I stepped out onto a graveled path as he emerged from the woods trailed by two great stags, their antlers barely missing trees on either side. As Mitch shoved out a hand to me, the stags turned to the forest, lowering their heads toward trailing gray shadows.

"A fitting honor guard," I commented.

"They felt I needed protection from your troops," he replied, jerking a thumb at six timber wolves hovering at the tree edge.

"Garm, Fenrir, take off. He's a friend," I said, addressing the two largest wolves. They glanced briefly at Mitch, then all six padded into the forest.

Inside, he settled his bulk into an oversized chair, taking the proffered Scotch. "You know this lake doesn't show on any map?" he said, downing the drink, "Not even those the Ministry of the Environment makes from satellite photos."

"Maybe the MOE needs better computers," I offered.

He glanced to where my array of computers resided. "Or better security on the systems they do have."

I shrugged, not rising to the bait.

Silence. He cleared his throat, staring out at the lake. "Speaking of security…"

"I hope you didn't fly up here to pitch that at me again," I interrupted. "I'm out. No more. You've plenty of predator class to recruit for your dirty little jobs."

He reddened.

"Besides," I continued, "Robbie runs security in the Circle. I doubt he'd be thrilled about this."

He said nothing, fixing me with the hot angry stare of the challenged bull. When he finally spoke, his voice was level. "Two years ago, Robert became active with an environmental protest group."

"So what? Lots of us are activists. It goes with the territory. I got Stelle into it. We used to try to recruit Robbie."

"Seen Robert lately?" he asked, too casually.

I snorted. "Mitch, I haven't talked to him or Stelle in eight years. What're you driving at? Is this about Robbie?"

He sighed and nodded, suddenly looking very old. I had never thought of him as old before.

"Gwyn," he said quietly, "Our Robert has threatened to kill two men. One is an important man, the type who attracts attention." He'd been looking at the empty glass in his hand. Now he looked up at me. "I need your help, Gwyn. To find Robbie first."

I shut up then and listened as Mitch told of the logging protests, the blockade, the protestors' deaths, and of Robbie's threat to kill Conrad and the truck driver. He talked and pleaded, pleaded and talked.

Finally, he paused. "There's something else," he said, staring out at the lake. "CSIS knows of this. According to our mole, somebody in CSIS is leaking intelligence on the Heroka to an outside party." He looked back to me. "Gwyn, we think someone's resurrected the Tainchel."

Involuntarily, I bared my teeth. Damn it. I questioned him on his source, what evidence he had, how recent was the tip, but he knew he had me. Finally, I'd agreed, because of the Tainchel angle, and because Robbie had been a friend and Mitch still was. That's what I'd told myself at the time. Now, watching the spirits dance in the firelight, I knew I'd done it for someone else.

Dance, spirits, dance.

Estelle and I had been an item for quite a while, back when I ran security in the northeast. For centuries, the Heroka were nothing more than creatures of legend. Security had mostly amounted to making sure things stayed that way. Then came the Tainchel, a covert operation of the federal intelligence agency CSIS, formed as we later learned, with the single goal of tracking down and capturing the Heroka. For scientific purposes.

Tainchel. Old Scottish term: Armed men advancing in a line through a forest to flush out and kill wolves.

We lost quite a few before we caught on. They'd developed specialized scanners from tests on early victims. Subtle differences in alpha wave patterns, infrared readings, and metabolic rates gave us away, even in crowded cities.

Then they got careless, and we became aware. I leaked word about a meeting that the Circle of the Heroka planned for an isolated spot. At the next full moon, of course. I figured they'd expect that.

Twenty of the Tainchel walked into the ambush, armed mostly with tranquilizer rifles. They didn't walk out. They'd encountered the Heroka before, but never predators. Wolves, bears, the big cats, birds of prey. We didn't take prisoners.

After, we contacted Justice and CSIS. I sent a list of the remaining Tainchel agents, present locations, recent activities, and a note saying, "We know who you are. We know where you are. We will kill to protect ourselves. Back off."

They backed off. CSIS disbanded the Tainchel, and an uneasy truce began.

The truce lasted. Estelle and I didn't. She argued against the ambush, the killings. I argued that we fought for our existence. In the end, we just argued.

Robert and I had been friends for years, and through me, he had come to know Estelle. After I exited the scene, the two of them became more than friends. About then, I resigned from the Circle. Robbie replaced me there too.

Dance, spirits. Dance with the beasts of the night.

Growling, Gelert turned toward a dim rustle in the forest. I gave the dog a mental command to lie down again. Stealth was not my intruder's aim. I stood as Leiddia stepped out of the trees, stopping at the edge of the firelight.

She smiled. "Hello again."

"Hi yourself."

"You don't seem surprised," she said as she approached.

"I had the feeling you wanted to tell me something."

"Yep," she said, "You're a wolf."

I tried to remain expressionless. "Excuse me?"

She walked to the opposite side of the fire and sat on the ground, grinning. "Blaidd. I looked it up. It's Welsh for wolf."

"Oh, right. I forgot I'd told you."

I sat again, as Gelert came over to nuzzle her. She took his huge head in both hands, rubbing him behind the ears. "And what's your name?"

I told her, and she made a face. "Gelert was the legendary hound of Prince Llewellyn of Wales," I explained.

"Hmm. So, why does Ed call you Grey Legs?"

I chuckled. "The Ojibwa and the Cree believe using its name will attract a wolf. So they call it Grey Legs, Grey Coat, Golden Tooth, Silent One. Ever since I told him what my name meant, he's called me that, as a joke."

She smiled again. "So he thinks you're a wolf, too."

I grinned back. In the store, I'd been so intent on her aura of the Mark, I'd overlooked how attractive she was. Gelert liked her too, always a good sign.

She stared at me. "You *are* a wolf."

I remained silent.

"What's it like," she asked, "to change, to be that way?"

"You do know, don't you? How?"

"Your friend, Robert. We met during the funerals at the church. Something about me fascinated him. He kept staring at me."

"Can't say I blame him."

"It wasn't that kind of interest, but thanks," she said smiling. "Anyway, I knew he was different too, but I didn't know what it was."

She shifted her gaze to the flames. "He was so upset, so sad. He said he had something to tell me, about me. That something must be added for what was lost. I didn't understand, but I wasn't afraid of him. Somehow, I knew I could trust him."

I smiled. That was Robbie—the size of a grizzly, but women treated him like a big teddy bear.

"At the cemetery after the burials, we walked together. We found a big stone just inside the forest, and sat and talked. Well, he talked. I just listened. He told me of the Heroka, of how you are a race older than man. How you each are linked to an animal species."

I nodded. "We have many names. The Ojibwa called us the Heroka, or Earth Spirits. They believed my people were ancestrally related to different animals, similar to totems. We bear traits and abilities of our totem animal, like keener senses, greater strength." I turned to Gelert. "And we can command those animals."

Without a word from me, Gelert trotted to my tent and emerged holding a cup in his mouth. He dropped it in my hand.

"Coffee?" I asked.

She laughed. "I guess house-training Gelert wasn't a problem. Thanks, just black is fine." She looked serious again. "Robert told me more."

I reached for the coffee pot hanging over the fire. "That we can change into our totem animals."

She nodded.

"You believed him?"

She took the cup from me. "Pretty well had to. He showed me."

I gave a low whistle. "He must have been sure about you."

"He said I had the right to know, that I had the Mark."

"Yes. Yes, you do," I said quietly.

"Then I'm one of you?" She leaned forward quickly, spilling coffee onto the ground.

I shook my head. "No. Not yet anyway. Very few with the Mark ever become one of the Heroka. They need assistance. Didn't Robert explain?"

"He had something to do first, something he owed someone. He was going away but said he'd be back to explain more and help me."

She got up then and walked to me slowly, as if trying not to frighten away an animal that had strayed in from the forest. She sat beside me, her leg brushing against mine, her breath cool and sweet on my face. I noticed something else.

"Your cheek," I began, reaching out.

She turned away. "He hit me."

"Your stepfather?"

She nodded.

I turned her face back to me with a finger on her chin. "Why?"

She looked down. "He was…touching me. I made him stop."

My hand squeezed her shoulder. "Has he tried this before?"

"No," she said with a sneer. "He's always saved his special attentions for Mom." She leaned against me, her head against my shoulder. "I hate him and I'm scared, Gwyn." Her voice was low but firm. "I wish I had your strength, your powers."

Wrapping my arms around her, I held her for a long time, neither of us speaking. Technically, I had to petition the Circle first, but I was never much on policy. To me, it was her right. I thought of her mom and Tom Barker. I thought of Tom with her.

"You'll have my powers," I said. "I'll give you your birthright."

She sat straight up. "You can do that? How?"

I grinned. "Well, there's the classical method or the modern approach, plus some, uh, variations. In the classical scenario, I shape shift and savagely attack you. Unique microorganisms in my saliva and in oils excreted from my claw tips enter your blood stream through your various wounds, meeting up with some equally unique enzymes that those with the Mark carry. This results in a mutated enzyme that modifies your cell structure. You're then of the Heroka, assuming you survive my attack."

She snuggled close again. "Well, I like where you attack me, but not the various wounds part."

"Chicken. Okay, the modern version then. I make an incision somewhere you don't mind having a scar, and apply a poultice moistened with my blood."

She wrinkled her nose. "Saliva, oils, blood. The Heroka don't practice safe shifting, do they?"

"We're immune to most human viral and bacterial infections, including AIDS. Some Heroka diseases exist, but they're treatable."

"Hoof and mouth disease?"

"Smart ass."

Leiddia laughed then looked thoughtful. "So I need to get certain of your bodily fluids into my bloodstream." She moved to rest her chin on my shoulder. "You mentioned variations?"

I stroked her hair. "They involve, uh, other bodily fluids."

She leaned forward, brushing her lips against mine. "And other methods of application?"

I nodded, pulling her to me into a long kiss. "So," I asked after a while, "which method would the patient prefer?"

"I'll try," she said, between kisses, "the variations."

Several variations later, we were both asleep.

I awoke alone except for Gelert, which wasn't what I'd had in mind. Over breakfast, I pondered whether I felt used.

She was a big girl. She'd known what she was after. She'd gotten it.

Used. I shrugged mentally. Not the first time.

Leaving Gelert to guard the plane, I broke camp and set out immediately for the driver's cabin. I wanted daylight to scout the area, and assure myself that this was not a trap.

Mitch and I had divided Robbie's two targets. Mitch had planned to cover Conrad in Toronto, while I watched the truck driver, since I'd lived here after Stelle and I split. That was our plan four days ago. Somehow, Robbie had known Conrad would be away from Toronto that night at his lodge in the Muskokas, and had killed him there. Once Mitch heard of Conrad's death, he'd head here, but Robbie had a full day on him.

It was up to me.

Sunlight filtered through the canopy of trees, warming the crisp fall day as I followed familiar forest trails. My thoughts kept drifting to Leiddia and last night.

Ed's map was clear, and I made good time, reaching a rise overlooking the cabin by early afternoon. Finding a spot with good cover and a clear view of the building, I watched, listened, and smelt the breeze. I repeated this process at three other locations before I was satisfied.

The driver was there, plus three men with rifles. Conrad's death had not gone unnoticed. I could detect no one else.

My plan was to intercept Robbie on his way to the cabin, away from the attention of the guards. My problem became figuring which route he'd take.

Three sides of the cabin were open field. Approaching undetected required coming in from behind, moving down through trees from the rise where I now stood. Under-growth choked most routes to the rise. The best path followed a forested ridge, where the forest floor was clear under the roof of trees.

I picked a spot giving a view of both the ridge and the fields surrounding the cabin, and downwind from the ridge path. After a snack of dried beef washed down with warm water, I settled behind a huge fallen tree to watch, wait, and sniff.

One hour. Darkness. Two hours. Moonrise. Four hours. Predators are used to waiting. I spent the time thinking of Leiddia. Her face and body kept shifting into Stelle's.

Midnight. The cry of a screech owl brought my head up. I shivered in the cold. The owl. A symbol of the souls of the dead in Indian myths. Shamans gave owl feathers to the dying to help them pass into the next world.

Just then, I caught a whiff. A minute later, I saw a huge shadow moving steadily along the ridge. For a moment, I thought I saw two shapes. Must have been the light. I watched long enough to guess his route, then moved to an intercept position.

Hidden, I listened. Twigs breaking, leaves rustling. Closer. Footsteps, breathing. I stepped out in front of him.

Startled, he stopped, dropping back into a defensive stance. Suddenly, I became aware of something some distance behind him. Something big and moving fast. And growling.

Shit. He'd brought help.

"Robbie! It's me, Gwyn!" The grizzly closed on me quickly, while I assessed the best tree to scale.

"Callisto! Halt!" Robbie's voice ripped the night. The huge beast rumbled to a stop at his side, snorted in my direction, then settled back on its great haunches.

Robbie was wearing jeans and hiking boots, and a denim jacket over a white T-shirt. He was bigger than I remembered. Reaching out to stroke the grizzly's hump, he looked me over. "Hello, wolf man. Been a long time."

"Too long, Robbie," I said, trying to sound more casual than I felt.

He seemed to think this over, scuffing the ground with a toe. "Come to help me finish?"

I shook my head.

"No. No, I didn't think so," he said sadly, then his face hardened. Pouncing with a speed belying his size, he caught me in the chest with his shoulder, knocking me to the ground.

I rolled and sprang to my feet. If he pinned me, it was over. We circled each other.

"Can't we talk?" I gasped, forcing air back into my lungs.

"Talking's done. We talked, we sang," he snarled, "we died. Now they die."

He tried a foot sweep. I backed away. Apparently, he was keeping his teddy out of it. Maybe he wanted a fair fight, which would be like him. Maybe he was worried I might have some reserves too. About then, I was wishing I'd thought of that.

Robert was a grappler, a wrestler. My style was karate — blocks and strikes. Not needing my hands to grasp meant I had an option he didn't. Staying in a left fighting stance, I moved my right hand closer to my body where my left arm hid it.

"You're not a killer, Robbie. Let it be."

Slowly. Concentrate. Keep circling. Gradually I felt it work. Now, I had to use it without killing him.

"Let it be? You mean, leave him to you. Well, he's mine, Gwyn. He dies by my hand, not yours."

I didn't get a chance to reply. He moved in, feinting a high punch, then dropped his shoulder and threw out an arm to circle my waist for a takedown. I sidestepped and blocked the arm, spinning him around and exposing his side. I drove in with my right hand, aiming for the shoulder.

A useless target for a normal strike. But not this strike.

Three inches of claws sank into flesh and muscle. A cheap shot. In tournaments, you must announce or display shifts. This wasn't a tournament.

He roared, spinning free but tearing open the wound. He stepped back groaning, left arm limp, useless. The grizzly growled but stayed put.

"It's over, Robbie," I said softly, shifting my hand back to normal.

He sank to his knees, head bowed. "Damn you…wanted to do it myself…she was mine too…," he muttered, then looked up. "Take me with you. It's not much farther. Let me see you do it." His face went dark. "I want to see him die, Gwyn."

"What the hell are you talking about? Nobody's killing any-body. What's with you? Stelle's going to flip! She hates killing. You're going to break her heart, man." *Like I did,* I thought.

He stared up at me, the strangest look on his face.

Something must be added for what was lost.

A chill filled my belly.

She was mine too.

"Gwyn," he said. His voice was gentle.

A lot of us are activists. I got Stelle into it.

"Stelle's dead. They killed her…"

A female protestor from out of town also died.

He dropped his head sobbing. I stood there, feeling like the leaves at my feet—brittle, broken, dead.

I got Stelle into it.

Mitch. He'd known, of course, but he needed me to stop Robbie. Isolated and estranged as I was from both Stelle and Robbie, he'd gambled on me not knowing. With one of the Heroka already out for revenge, he knew that if he told me, I'd be racing Robbie to the kill.

Now I did know. So what was I going to do?

Standing there, I realized that I'd always thought Stelle and I would get back together somehow, sometime. I had never stopped loving her, never believed it was over. I shook my head, fighting the anger and the tears. Too much killing, she had said. I knew what she'd say now.

"Come on, Robbie," I said quietly. "Let's go home."

I'll never know who their first target really was. They must have held back after I appeared, hoping we'd kill each other. When we stopped fighting, they stopped waiting.

I had just knelt to help Robbie up, when the bullet caught him in the bad shoulder. He took another in the chest before I pulled him to the ground and threw myself flat. I looked back in the direction of the cabin. A line of figures was moving toward us through the trees. Figures with guns.

The Tainchel.

"How many?" he gasped.

"Too many."

"Those aren't trank guns," he groaned.

"I think they've given themselves a new mandate." They'd be on us in seconds, but I couldn't leave Robbie behind.

"Just...bought you...some time," Robbie gasped. The next second I knew what he meant.

Sixteen hundred pounds of furred fury burst from a thicket. Charging into the nearest group, it grabbed a man in its jaws and threw him against a tree. Rearing up three meters on hind legs, Callisto sent two more spinning through the air with a slashing swipe of her paw.

I watched transfixed. "Run, Gwyn," Robbie said. "You can't save me."

I shook my head. Bodies at her feet, Callisto turned to charge another cluster. More fell before her. The rest were firing at the grizzly but still she attacked. The shooting continued, and she was slowing. Rushing another man, she reared to her full height and fell on her screaming victim. She didn't rise.

Robbie sobbed quietly.

They put more shots into her. Silence followed. No movement. Callisto had made them cautious. She'd bought us time.

Robbie was pale, breathing in rapid gasps. The Indians believed the bear possessed great curative powers. Robbie needed more than legends.

I called out. "Listen to me! I'll make this easy. Get my friend medical help, and I'll surrender." Robbie shook his head violently, prompting a coughing fit.

Nothing.

"No deals," a voice finally replied, "and no prisoners!"

The firing started again, heavier this time. Keeping my head down, I started to concentrate on a shift. It was our last chance. They wanted blood.

Robbie grabbed my arm just as I sensed them. Too late. Something crashed down on my skull, and I slumped forward, stunned. Fighting for control, I managed to turn my head to look behind me.

Two men. Two rifles.

The firing from in front of us stopped. These two had used that sound cover to sneak up behind us. Focusing on my shift had dulled my other senses.

"Silver bullet time, freak," said the closest one. Grinning, he raised his rifle.

With a roar, a gray mass hurtled out of the shadows. Huge jaws closed on the man's neck with a sickening snap. A black blur pulled down the other gunman. Around us, the Tainchel screamed and cursed, dark forms leaping at them from all sides.

My puppy had arrived, and he'd brought friends.

Gelert shoved his face into mine, licking and whining. I could smell blood. Throwing an arm over his great back, I pulled myself up and looked around.

The wolves outnumbered the Tainchel, but the men had guns, and their initial shock was wearing off. The survivors were in a clump, backs to each other, firing outwards. My gray brothers were falling, dying. Dying for me.

I shifted. The Black Wolf came among them.

I came out of it with Gelert nuzzling my face. A dozen wolves clustered around me, wagging their tails or licking wounds. Pain screaming from a dozen places, I rose stiffly but found no major damage.

I remember little after a shift. Walking around, counting the dead, I figured it was just as well. Six wolves, eighteen of the Tainchel. No human survivors. Naked and freezing, my clothes shredded from the shift, I stripped one of the less bloody bodies for garments.

I found him lying against a tree, deathly white, soaked in blood. I knelt beside him. "Robbie?"

His eyes focused on me. "Gwyn...," he whispered, "there's a girl...Leiddia..."

"I know. She's one of us now."

He smiled. "You and I…always finding the same woman." The smile faded. "Stelle…never stopped loving you. Sometimes…I hated you for that. Sorry." His eyes closed.

I swallowed hard. "Robbie, sometimes I hated you for being with her. I'm sorry too."

No reply.

"Robbie?"

I felt for a pulse, but I knew. I could smell it. The Bear was dead. I wondered if he'd heard me.

In a nearby clearing away from the trees, I built a low bier from rocks, piling it with dried branches. I dragged him over and with a great struggle lifted him on top. Beside him, I placed my dead wolven brethren. Callisto, too huge to move, I covered with rocks.

A search of the bodies provided matches. As I returned, a great horned owl lifted up from the bier into the night. A single feather lay on Robbie's chest. I held it for a moment, then tucked it into his shirt.

I lit the wood and stood back as the fire caught quickly, roaring with the rising wind. Turning from the flames and smoke, I stopped, surrounded.

Black bears, wolves, coyotes, foxes, animals of all kinds encircled the pyre. Gelert began a mournful howl, picked up by the wolves. The other animals joined with growls, roars, and snarls.

Howl, beasts of the night. Howl for our fallen. Howl over the bodies of our foes.

I walked away through smoke and mist and trees, Gelert at my side, until we stood looking down at the driver's cabin. The guards pointed up the hill at the glow of the fire.

One task remained. They had killed my woman. They had killed my friend. Gelert growled.

I began to shift. A wolf howled.

No prisoners.

Ed was behind the counter when I came into the store the next afternoon. He looked up but didn't smile. "Made up some supplies for you."

"How'd you know I'd be heading out?"

He said nothing, but pushed the newspaper forward. I read the front page. The bodies had been found already.

"You'd better go, Gwyn."

I looked up. He had turned his back. Taking the supplies, I placed more money than required on the counter.

As I moved to the door, he spoke again, his back still to me. "Tom Barker was at the hospital last night. Cut up real bad. That nurse Vera knows said it looked like he'd fought a wild cat and lost." He turned to look at me. "He's left them. Says he's not going back."

"Probably for the best," I said quietly.

"Yeah. Assuming they can support themselves," he replied, an edge to his voice.

I walked to the door, not looking back.

"Guess there's one more beast in the night now," he said under his breath. I'm not sure if he meant me to hear. As I stepped outside, I felt that Ed was making a warding sign, a sign to keep away the beasts of the night. I hoped I was wrong.

It is night now. I sit in my camp and stare as the spirits dance in my fire. Feel their heat on my body. Feel my body an empty shell, hollow. Wait for the fire spirits to bake it hard. Wait for the animal cry in the night to shatter this shell, crumble it to dust. Listen to the wind that will blow the dust, scatter me, send me away.

Stelle is dead. Robbie is dead. I am dead too. Perhaps I have been dead these past fifteen years.

The wind stirs the ashes, dancing the flames. Gelert raises his mighty head to stare into the darkness. The fire crackles. A branch snaps behind me. I turn to see liquid night flow feline from the trees toward me. It shifts. It changes. Twin emerald fires melt to gray green eyes. Paws become hands. Paws become feet. Ebony fur fades to the pale smoothness of her skin, streams to the black cascade of her hair. Naked, she stands before me, cat-beast of the night now woman again.

I walk to her slowly, as if trying not to frighten away an animal that has strayed in from the forest. Wrapping my coat about her, I stare at her searching for something there to fill this empty shell, and she endures it.

"Then it worked," I finally say.

"It worked," she replies, a sound with the breeze. She touches my cheek, tracing a line with a long sharp nail. "I need a teacher."

"I need," I begin, before my throat strangles the words and the tears flow. "I need much more than that."

She whispers, "I love you," as we lie down by the fire, and I say I love her too. I hope one day we can mean it when we say it, as I fill her emptiness, and she begins to fill mine.

After, I watch her sleep by the dying ember light. Stelle is dead. Robbie is dead. But another of the Heroka lies beside me. The spirits do not dance. For now, it is enough.

Story Notes

This was my first story. The first one I wrote. The first one I sold. I received the acceptance letter on December 31, which was a great way to end a year and start a new one. "Spirit Dance" sold to the Canadian anthology, *Tesseracts6*, edited by famed Canadian SF author, Robert J. Sawyer, and his wife, the poet, Carolyn Clink.

"Spirit Dance" was a finalist for the Aurora Award the year after it came out and has since been reprinted two dozen times, in seventeen languages and twenty countries. A French translation won the Aurora Award in 2001.

If you enjoyed this tale, I have another Heroka story available as an ebook: "A Bird in the Hand" (which appeared in the anthology *Warrior Wisewoman 3* in 2010). A third story, "Dream Flight," has only been published in French so far, in my collection *La Danse des Esprits*.

My novel, *The Wolf at the End of the World*, is based on "Spirit Dance." In it, we again meet up with Gwyn, Gelert, Leiddia, Ed, Mitch, and the Tainchel, and Gwyn encounters more shadows from his past. I've included the opening chapter to that novel at the end of this book.

Going Down
to Lucky Town

If the friends and enemies of Charles Tobias Perlman could agree on one thing, it was this—you *never* bet against Charlie the Pearl.

Ever.

And if his enemies numbered higher than his friends, well, Charlie just put it down to the life he had lived. A life that did not appear, at that particular moment, as if it would be lived much longer.

He lay in the dirt behind the Canadian National Exhibition in Toronto on a beautiful August evening of 1967. His mouth was bleeding and his head throbbing from the beating just delivered by Eddie Fenton, his former partner-in-crime who was now taking out a gun.

Reaching down, Eddie pulled the big pearl stickpin from Charlie's tie. He polished it with a couple of rubs on his paisley shirt, then stuck it in the lapel of his dirty denim jacket.

Charlie looked up at him, licking blood from his lips. "That," he commented, "looks ridiculous."

"Shaddup." Eddie aimed the revolver at Charlie's head. "Payback time, old man. Looks like my lucky day."

Recent events ran through Charlie's head faster than a drugged filly. He spat out a broken tooth and chuckled. "Kid, you know absolutely *nothing* about luck."

Eddie laughed. "And you do? Lying bleeding in the dirt and about to eat a bullet?" He pulled back the hammer with a click that sounded like two dice knocking together. "You got nothing left to teach me, pops."

With an amazing degree of detachment, Charlie watched Eddie's finger tighten on the trigger. "Trust me, kid," Charlie said quietly, "I'm about to give you one last lesson."

It had all started four weeks ago.

Well, no, that's not quite right. In truth, it had started thirty-two years ago. Charlie had been just fifteen when the winds of the dust bowl had swept his parents from his life, like a croupier raking in losing bets. He'd hit the road then, leaving behind two white crosses planted in the family farm in Oklahoma, the only things to rise from that dead earth in two years.

Charlie had spent the rest of the thirties traveling the Midwest, working as a carnie, until William "Papa" Dernstead, an itinerant gambler and con artist, took him under his wing, teaching Charlie the tricks of what became his trade. Papa

Bill had died two years later, amazingly of natural causes, but Charlie's road through life had been laid before him—part-time gambler, part-time con man, and full-time observer of human nature and benefitor thereof.

His less charitable enemies explained their losing encounters with Charlie by claiming that he was lucky. Just plain lucky. Lucky to have beaten them. Lucky to still be alive.

His friends and his more dangerous enemies knew better. They knew that you didn't live as long as Charlie had, doing what Charlie did, just by being lucky. You had to know your game, know people, know when to zig and when to zag. In short, you had to be good.

So was Charlie good or lucky? Well, as in most cases, the truth lay in those spaces in between. Charlie the Pearl was very good at being very lucky.

Charlie could *see* luck.

Whether it was a four-year-old in the fifth at Woodbine or a pale-faced housewife at the craps table in Vegas, Charlie could look at them in a certain way—kind of sideways, from an angle—and he could see the luck on them, if any was there to be seen. And luck always looked the same way to Charlie.

Sparkly.

Which was why, four weeks ago, he had found himself planning a visit to Waterloo, a small southern Ontario town as unexceptional as most small southern Ontario towns, except that it was currently, if he was reading the signs correctly, probably the luckiest place on Earth. And Charlie planned to cash in on that luck.

However, a week later, he was still in Toronto, because his travel plans required first ridding himself of his current partner, a twitchy young psychopath named Eddie Fenton.

Charlie didn't normally choose twitchy young psychopaths as partners, but in fairness to Charlie, Eddie had at first exhibited only the twitchiness and youth. Unfortunately, the psychopath didn't take long to emerge.

"Bloody hell, you killed him." Charlie was whispering, as if a raised voice might attract more attention than the three shots that Eddie had just pumped into the man now lying dead in the alley.

"That was the idea," Eddie said, pulling a bloody envelope from the man's jacket. Charlie caught a flash of the sheaf of hundreds inside. "Let's go." Eddie walked to the end of the alley and casually stepped onto the street. Charlie swallowed, and then with another look at the body, he hurried to catch up.

Eddie handed a wad of bills to Charlie as they walked. "Here's your half." Stuffing the rest in his pocket, he lit a cigarette.

Charlie took the money in a shaking hand. He knew it was far less than half, but he was suddenly too scared of Eddie to complain. "Why'd you kill him?" he croaked. "Another minute, and I would've switched the envelopes."

Eddie shrugged. "What's your beef? We wanted the money. We got the money."

And an innocent albeit greedy man is dead, Charlie thought. A man Charlie had picked as the perfect mark. He swallowed, trying to swallow his guilt too, but his throat constricted. And in that moment, Charlie made up his mind.

Eddie had to go.

Eddie took a drag on his cigarette. "So what's our next score, old man?"

A very frightened Charles Perlman grinned his fear away as Charlie the Pearl took control. "Kid, I've got the perfect mark." As Charlie outlined their next con, the only thing he left out was that this time the mark was going to be Eddie.

The Yonge Street Strip that evening was jammed with teenagers from the suburbs, hippies from Yorkville, gawking tourists, and the normal assortment of lowlifes that lived off teenagers, hippies and gawking tourists. Charlie and Eddie sat at an outdoor patio, watching the parade of mini skirts, tie-dyes, and bell-bottoms. The Beatles pumped the air from a jukebox inside, greeting everyone within earshot with "Hello Goodbye," which Charlie found extremely appropriate.

Eddie dropped his eyes as two burly policemen passed by on the street. He flicked a cigarette butt away. "Awful lot of cops."

"They're looking for dealers, teenagers doing dope, drunks, fights," Charlie said, exuding confidence. "They won't even notice us."

"So when's this mark showing up?" Eddie said, looking around dubiously.

He already has, Charlie thought, smiling at Eddie. "Let me check inside. Maybe he's waiting for us in there." Charlie got up. As he passed behind Eddie, Charlie slipped a wallet into the outside pocket of Eddie's jacket.

The wallet didn't belong to Eddie. It didn't belong to Charlie. Up until a few minutes ago, it had belonged to a man at the bar inside the restaurant, until Charlie had obtained it as he brushed by the man on his way to the patio.

Charlie went back inside. The man was still at the bar, but was now frantically searching his pockets and trying to explain his problem to a beefy and unsympathetic bartender.

"Excuse me, sir" Charlie said with his most innocent look. "Have you lost your wallet?"

Relief washed over the man's face. "Yes! Did you find one?"

"No, but I believe I know what happened to yours. You see, when I came in I saw a man bump against you. I believe he picked your pocket. He's on the patio now. In the far corner. Jeans, white t-shirt." Charlie watched as the bartender and the man picked out Eddie on the patio. "There's a couple of cops outside," Charlie added helpfully. "Would you like me to get them?"

An hour later, with Eddie in jail and unable to make bail, Charlie was in his car, a big black '62 Impala that drove like a boat, on the road to Waterloo, finally chasing the luck he knew was there. About thirty minutes out from Toronto on the 401, he saw the sign "Guelph exit—2 miles." After a moment's hesitation, he moved over to the right-hand lane.

In 1949 in Guelph, Charlie had met Mary, his greatest love and greatest regret. Charlie had never planned to marry or to have a family. Hell, Charlie had never planned any of his life. He'd just played the cards he'd been dealt, happy to still be sitting at the table rather than lying under it. But no one had ever explained to Charlie that there were things in life that you couldn't plan for—or against —and that falling in love was one of them.

That first year, he had lain in bed each night beside his young wife and prayed to a god he didn't believe in. At first, Charlie prayed for the strength to be a good husband. Near the end, he prayed just for the strength to stay one more day. His love for Mary and the promises he had made kept him by her side through that first winter. But spring brought a traveling carnival to town, and when it left, it took Charlie with it.

He never knew he had a daughter until one of Mary's letters caught up with him two years later. Inside was a picture. Her name was Brighid, and she was redheaded and adorable, and when Charlie first saw her, he lost his heart for the second and last time in his life.

But by then Charlie knew himself a little better. He knew that even a daughter wouldn't change the man he was, and that even if he went back intending to stay, he'd eventually leave again. He made it a point to pass through town at least once a year. Mary always took him back, into her house and her bed. She never asked him to stay. Charlie figured that by then she knew him a little better too.

Charlie hadn't seen Mary or Brighid in over a year, not since Brighid had turned sixteen. So when the exit for Guelph came, Charlie took it, because he missed the two girls in his life. An hour later, he learned that he'd missed something else that past year.

The cemetery was empty except for the two of them. The sun was hot on her back, but Brighid felt cold. Charlie stood head down, before Mary's grave. Brighid watched him, searching her feelings for some remnant of the boundless love and adulation she used to hold for this man, this stranger.

Brighid had been only three when she'd come to understand that she had her daddy for only a few days every year. She and her mom had learned to make the most out of those rare moments of pretending to be a family. But as Brighid grew older, she noticed that her father's visits brought something else with them. Sometimes, especially when Brighid begged Charlie to tell her another story of his life on the road, she saw a fear in her mom's eyes.

She'd asked her mom about it once. Brighid had been ten at the time.

Mary had hesitated. "I guess, sweetheart," she had replied finally, "I've always been afraid that there's a little too much of your father in you." She'd reached out then, brushing Brighid's soft fine hair back from her face and stroking her cheek. "You'd never let him take you from me, would you? I've learned to live with losing him each year. I couldn't live with losing you."

Brighid had hugged her mom then and promised that she'd never leave her alone. It never occurred to Brighid that Mary might be the one who would be leaving.

Charlie turned from Mary's grave finally and walked back to Brighid. He cleared his throat. "I hope…I hope she didn't suffer."

Brighid snorted. "She had cancer. What the fuck do you think?"

Charlie stared at her open-mouthed. She'd never talked to him that way before.

"She suffered, Charlie," Brighid snapped, her voice rising with her anger, anger that she'd nursed since Mary's death. "She was in pain all day, every day. And there wasn't one of those days that she didn't ask for you." She was screaming at him now. "Not a single fucking day that she didn't ask for the man she still loved for god knows what reason because I sure as fuck wouldn't have anymore."

Charlie reddened. "Bee, I didn't even know she—"

"I wrote you, Charlie. Every week, to every fucking address you'd given us."

"I've been moving around—"

"Oh, god, that's new," she cried, throwing up her hands. "Moving around. A new place all the time for Charlie the Pearl. You're fucking everywhere, aren't you? Everywhere except here. You should've…" Her words caught in her throat as her anger washed away with her tears. "You should have been *here,* Charlie." Her voice trailed off, and she stood there, hugging herself, sobbing, staring at him.

Charlie looked at the ground, not meeting her eyes. "You used to call me Daddy," he said finally.

"My daddy would've been here," she said and began walking to the car. "Take me back."

They drove in silence. Brighid sat slumped in the seat, staring out the window. She could feel Charlie's eyes on her whenever he looked over. When he finally spoke, his voice held none of his usual confidence. "That place I found you…I mean, what is it? Why are you there?"

"It's a group home," she said, her voice a monotone. She felt dead inside. "I'm a ward of the province until I turn eighteen. They're trying to find me foster parents."

Charlie swallowed, shooting her a look. "But I'm your parent."

"I told them I didn't have a father." Brighid enjoyed seeing him flinch at that. She didn't mention that she'd done her very best so far to scare away any potential set of parents that the administrator had put in front of her.

And in that moment, Brighid admitted that, despite all the anger that her seventeen-year-old self harbored for Charlie, a little girl still lived inside her who had been praying for her daddy to come home. Praying that this wild vagabond would once again appear like magic, telling her stories of the road that made her laugh and forget her troubles and want to travel that road with him.

Brighid sat waiting for Charlie to do his magic, to say the words that would somehow make her world all right again. But they drove the rest of the way to the group home in silence. Charlie pulled up to the curb. Fighting back another bout of tears, Brighid reached for the door.

Charlie finally spoke. "Bee, it's no life for a girl, you know."

She took her hand off the door handle and turned back to him. What was he talking about?

"I mean, I can barely support myself let alone…" His voice trailed off. He looked at her.

Despite herself, she grinned. She'd always been able to figure Charlie out faster than Mary had. "So I'll help. You taught me lots of stuff."

Charlie shook his head. "I don't know. I guess we could try it for a while, but…"

"Let me get some things," she said before he could finish. She jumped out of the car and ran up the steps of the home, her anger forgotten. There'd be no foster home for her. All her life she had dreamed of this, of travelling with Charlie, of being part of his stories instead of just listening to them.

But later, as they drove out of town, with Charlie telling one of those stories and Brighid laughing, they passed the cemetery again. Charlie didn't give it a second glance, but Brighid felt a pang of guilt. As she watched Mary's resting place fall behind them, she wondered if maybe her mom hadn't been right all along.

Maybe there was a bit too much of Charlie in her after all.

"So let me get this straight," Brighid said as Charlie drove, "You're chasing some strange streak of *luck*?"

He looked over at her, still conflicted about bringing her along. Everything he'd ever learned told him this was the dumbest move he'd ever made. But everything he felt said that he was doing the right thing. He couldn't leave her with some strangers in a foster home. Still, this was no life for a girl. Sure, he could look out for her while he was here, but he'd always known that his kind of life wouldn't be a long one. So that meant he needed one big score, enough to set her up for a while, enough to get through university. To get her own life. Then he could go on with his, alone, knowing she was safe. On the other hand, it *was* nice having her around...

He sighed. He was letting his heart trump his head. Always a bad move.

He nodded. "I noticed it about a month ago in Sarnia. News reports about weird occurrences, like long-lost triplets discovering each other for the first time. An entire foursome scoring a hole-in-one. Three people at a rec club getting a perfect hand in cribbage on the same day. Weird stuff."

"And your *sparkly* alarm went off," she said. "That thing that lets you *see* luck."

Charlie nodded. "So I check into it, right? And I find more weirdness. A complete bowling team throws perfect games—twice. The longest shots on the board at the local track win every race that day. And guess where the Irish Sweepstakes winner and every Publisher's Clearing House winner that month lived?"

"So why're we going to Waterloo instead of Sarnia?"

"The luck stopped in Sarnia. But I knew something was up, so I kept watching the news. And sure enough, a couple of days later, the weirdness started in London. After about a month, it moved to Waterloo."

"So...luck is taking a tour of Ontario?" she asked, one eyebrow raised.

"And moving east, it appears," Charlie said.

Charlie and Brighid spent a fruitless day driving around Waterloo while Charlie looked for 'anything sparkly.' Dinnertime found them in an A&W on Columbia Avenue not far from the University of Waterloo. Despite their lack of success, Brighid was having the time of her life, relishing Charlie's undivided attention and her first day on 'the road.'

Still, she could tell Charlie was frustrated, and she didn't want him to begin thinking that bringing her along had been a bad idea, that somehow she was bad luck.

"You know," Brighid said between bites of her burger, "it's great that you can see lucky people, but wouldn't it be better if we knew where to look?"

"Suggestions?"

"Well, if there are sparklies in town, wouldn't they use their luck to cash in?" She pushed a flyer that had been on their table towards him. He read it.

KITCHENER-WATERLOO AGRICULTURAL FAIR
AUGUST 1-4
RIDES, GAMES, CRAFTS, HORTICULTURAL DISPLAYS
ANIMAL JUDGING, TRACTOR PULL

Charlie shrugged. "So?"

She pointed to the last line on the flyer.

CHARITY CASINO
ALL PROCEEDS TO EASTER SEALS SOCIETY

He looked up at her. "And it's just down the road."

"Told you I could help," she said with a grin.

Charlie strolled through the fairgrounds, Brighid by his side, his search for the mysterious source of luck momentarily forgotten, drowned in a flood of memories.

In the center of the midway, he stopped and closed his eyes, breathing in the smells of candy floss and popcorn and ice cream waffles as the sounds of the fair washed over him—the cries of the barkers at the games, the clatter of the rollercoaster, the screams of the riders. This world was part of him and always would be.

"This reminds me of when you took me to the Ex, Daddy," Brighid said from beside him.

He opened his eyes and grinned at her. She'd started calling him 'Daddy' again. The 'Ex' was the Canadian National Exhibition, held each year in Toronto in late August. "I remember."

She squeezed his hand. "You just showed up one day, unexpected as always, and we drove into Toronto in that old blue Pontiac of yours. You seemed to know every carnie on every ride and every game."

Charlie laughed. "I don't think they let us pay for anything that entire day."

"That was one of the happiest days of my life," she said, putting her arm around his waist as they walked. "You used to be a carnie, didn't you?"

He nodded. "Yep. All my teen years. Never had much money, but I made the best friends I've ever known." He smiled. "Those were the happiest days of *my* life," he said, and regretted it immediately. "I mean, till mom and you came along," he added.

Brighid dropped her arm from his waist, her smile gone. "Uh huh." She nodded to a big white tent. "There's the casino," she said and began walking towards it without waiting for him.

He sighed. "Nicely done, Charlie," he muttered to himself as he followed her. They walked inside. And Charlie gasped.

The tent was filled with sparkly people. They gambled at the blackjack tables and the roulette wheel, lounged at the bar, clustered in clumps of conversations. And everywhere they sparkled. More than sparkled. They shone. Glowed. Burnt like bipedal suns.

Charlie was stunned. "My god," he said. "We've found it. So many. It's all so...so..."

"Sparkly?" Brighid offered.

He rubbed his eyes. "Bright. Too bright. It's everywhere. Don't know why, but everyone here's running hotter than a pair of loaded dice. Everyone's—" He stopped. "Actually," he said slowly, "not *quite* everyone."

A man sat at a table, looking very out of place. Not because he was alone or was the only person apparently not having a wonderful time, although both were true.

No, he stood out because, in a room full of the brightest sparkly people Charlie had ever seen, this guy was a people-shaped piece of the night. To Charlie's sparkly vision, the man looked as if he'd spray-painted himself black and then, just in case he'd missed any spots, taken a swim in an oil spill.

"Bee," Charlie said, "I think I just figured something out."

"You found the luck?" she replied.

"Something even better," Charlie said as he walked towards the man.

To Brighid, the man seemed too old to be a university student, maybe mid-thirties. He was thin, almost gaunt, with long, unkempt, black hair, and dressed as if he shopped in second-hand stores that never had his size. He huddled more than sat at the table, flanked now by Charlie and Brighid, like a canary trapped between two cats.

"You see," Charlie was explaining, over a beer he'd bought that the man wasn't drinking, "Luck isn't some mathematical concept. It's not probabilities and standard deviations. It's tangible, like a natural element, as much a part of our world as air." Charlie paused. "Actually, more like water. Cuz we all have air to breathe, right? But water's not so democratic. Oceans and lakes some places, deserts other places. Floods here, droughts there. Somewhere right now, somebody's having a nice swim while somewhere else, some poor sucker is dying of thirst. Likewise, somewhere, some lucky bastard is on the biggest winning streak of his life, while some poor sap just lost everything on a 'sure thing'."

Charlie nodded at the nearest blackjack table. "It's like there's a glass of luck on that table. Maybe tonight everyone'll take a small sip, or maybe somebody'll drink the whole thing, and the rest will go thirsty. Winners and losers. Luck doesn't care which of us is which. Except," Charlie stopped, and looked back at the man, "when *you're* around."

"How'd you find me?" the man asked, resignation in his voice, as if he'd played this scene before.

Charlie shrugged. "Let's just say I can see the people with a full glass of water. You, on the other hand, are like the Sahara Desert."

"Enough with the water analogies. You're going to make me pee," Brighid said, struggling to follow Charlie. "What's going on?"

"This gentleman," Charlie said, "has absolutely no luck on him at all. And somehow…" Charlie shrugged. "…don't know how…but somehow, he's creating ever so much good luck for everyone in his immediate vicinity."

With shaking hands, the man pushed his chair back. "You can't make me do anything."

"Hey, fella," Charlie said. "We just wanted—"

"You can't make me," the man said, standing up. He started to turn away.

"You've been used," Brighid said, suddenly understanding the fear she saw in the man's face. Charlie looked at her in surprise.

The man stopped. Brighid smiled up at him. "You've been used. By people like us. People who figured it out, wanted to use you to give themselves a big score."

The man looked at Brighid, and she could tell that he was seeing somebody else in her face. He considered her for a moment longer, then nodded. "Yeah. I've been used."

Brighid patted the chair beside her. "Why don't you tell us about it? Maybe we can help." The man sat down, and she allowed herself a flush of pride as she saw Charlie giving her a silent thumbs-up signal.

The man spoke in a slow, quiet monotone that Charlie had to strain to hear over the crowd. His name was Jim. He wouldn't give a last name. Said that he was afraid of people finding him.

"It started a year ago," Jim said. "Head-on collision with a drunk driver. I was hurt pretty bad. Constant headaches after, but I told myself that at least I survived. The other driver died. It wasn't long before I was wishing that I'd died too.

"Things started happening to me. Weird, improbable stuff at first, then it got worse. And for every bad thing that happened to me, something wonderful happened to somebody around me. I get fired, and my neighbor, who hasn't worked in three years, replaces me. I have to sell our house just when the real estate market bottoms out. My cousin buys it, and a month later it doubles in value. My wife leaves me for my brother, and a week later she gets this big inheritance." Jim shook his head. "It was everywhere, all the time. Every part of my life. Finally, I couldn't take it anymore. I tried to kill myself." Jim looked at them both. "*It* wouldn't let me."

Charlie and Brighid exchanged looks. "Um…*it*?" Charlie asked, suddenly developing a very bad feeling about all of this.

Jim grabbed Charlie's arm in a grip that made Charlie wince. "*It*." He swallowed. "There's *something* inside me."

"Some—*thing*?" Charlie asked, shooting Brighid a look. She gave him an 'I don't get it either' palms up shrug.

Jim nodded so fast Charlie thought his head would fall off. Suddenly animated, the words began rushing out of him. "You're right about luck," Jim said. "It *is* tangible. But luck—there are two kinds, see—good and bad. Everybody has some of both. Sometimes we have more good than bad. Those times, we're lucky. Good things happen to us. But, sometimes it's the other way around, and then…bad things happen." He shook his head.

"And you have this…thing?" Charlie asked, wishing he wasn't having this conversation. "Inside you?"

Jim nodded, then shivered.

"Uh, what kind of thing, Jim?" Charlie asked.

Jim shook his head. "Don't know. But it's *hungry*. All the time."

"Hungry?" Brighid asked. "For what?"

Inside the mind of Charlie the Pearl, the penny dropped. "For bad luck," he said. Brighid frowned. Jim almost looked relieved. "Jeez, that's it," Charlie said. "You don't give people *good* luck. Somehow you suck all the *bad* luck out of them."

Jim shook his head, agitated again. "I don't. This thing inside me does."

Charlie nodded. "Yeah, sure." He flashed Brighid a wink. "This, uh, thing eats all the bad luck in everyone around you." Charlie looked at all the sparkly people. "No wonder they're lucky. All they've got left is *good* luck."

"And all I've got is bad luck," Jim said, slumping back again.

"So bad you tried to kill yourself," Brighid said softly. She put her hand on his arm.

"Tried and tried," he said, smiling sadly at her. "But it won't let me. Something always prevents me from doing it. The gun misfires. The rope breaks. I throw up the poison." He shook his head. "I've tried stepping in front of buses, drowning, electrocution, slashing my wrists. Something always saves me."

Charlie was puzzled. "Sounds more like good luck than bad."

Jim chuckled softly. "It needs to keep me alive. Otherwise, it can't feed." He looked at their faces, then shrugged. "You don't believe me. But I know—it's inside me."

"So then the good luck for people around you is just a side effect?" Brighid asked.

Jim nodded. "This thing couldn't care less about them. It just wants their bad luck. That's why I have to get to Toronto."

"Not sure I'm following you there, Jim," Charlie said, becoming more and more concerned that his pot of luck at the end of this rainbow was turning out to be a complete whack job.

"My daughter has cancer," Jim said quietly.

Brighid put her hand to her mouth, and Charlie knew that she was thinking of Mary.

"Her name's Anne," Jim said, looking at Brighid with a sad smile. "You remind me of her. She's fifteen. She lives in Toronto now with her mom, and she's the only thing I still love in this world." His smile disappeared. "The doctors say there's nothing more they can do, but I *know* that if I can get to her," he said, straightening up, "then I can make this thing inside me work *for* me for once. Don't you see? If I was near Anne, I'd pull all the bad luck out of her, and she'd get well again."

Brighid nodded. "So that's why you've been moving east. Towards Toronto."

Charlie rubbed his chin. "Been moving kind of slowly, haven't you, Jimbo? Why not just hop on a bus or train?"

Jim laughed, a bitter empty sound. "What do you think? Bad luck. Weird things keep preventing me from getting there. Plus I've run out of money."

"So why're you in a casino?" Charlie asked. "You can't bet and if you did, you wouldn't win."

Jim shrugged. "But I make other people win. And winners tend to be generous to beggars, which is all I am now. But I still don't have enough for bus fare to Toronto. "

"Don't you worry," Brighid said. "We'll help you get to your daughter."

"Uh, Bee," Charlie said, forcing a smile, "could I please have a word alone with you?" He stood up, taking Brighid by the arm. "Be right back, Jimbo."

Pulling Brighid over to a relatively quiet corner, he glared at her. "C'mon, Bee. You believe him? That he has some kind of demon-monster-whatever-thingy inside him that lives on bad luck? The guy's on a losing streak and just wants a free ride home. Jeez, I thought I taught you how not to be a mark."

She reddened. Looking back to where Jim sat slumped, she bit her lip. "Well, that thingy-inside-him bit is hard to swallow. But you picked him out as the only non-sparkly here."

Charlie nodded. "That part I buy, cuz I can see it. Don't know how it works. Don't care. All I know is that this guy makes anybody around him very, very lucky."

She folded her arms. Always a bad sign. "And you plan to cash in on him?"

Charlie spread his hands. "Why not? We wouldn't be hurting him."

"We wouldn't be helping, either," she said. "What about his daughter? If you really believe he can make us lucky, then he might be right about saving her just by being there."

Charlie rubbed his chin. "Okay," he said, "we'll take him to Toronto." Brighid brightened. "And," he added, "we help ourselves at the same time."

They made Jim a deal. They'd drive him to Toronto and his daughter, if he'd accompany Charlie to the horse racing tracks along the way, where Jim's proximity would ensure Charlie of a winning ticket with every bet.

Jim looked suspicious. "And you'll let me go after? You won't try to...keep me?"

"Keep you?" Brighid said. "You mean, like a prisoner? People have actually tried to do that?"

Jim nodded, and Charlie shook his head, feigning disgust with the human race and pretending that the same idea hadn't occurred to him. Jim smiled, an expression as out of place on his sad face as an honest dollar in Charlie's pocket. "Looks like my luck is finally starting to change."

Brighid grinned and squeezed his arm. Charlie forced a smile, thinking of the big score he needed to make sure that Brighid was safe and secure in life. The last thing he wanted was for Jim's luck to change.

I think we lost them," Brighid said, staring out the back window of Charlie's big black Impala as they barreled down Highway 427 and away from Woodbine Racetrack.

Charlie checked the rear-view mirror, then eased off the accelerator a bit and shifted lanes to take the ramp for the Gardiner Expressway into downtown Toronto. "I guess winning on the longest shot for ten races in a row attracted a little attention to ourselves."

"You got greedy," Brighid said. "The thing you told me never to do."

"You are so right, daughter of mine. But don't worry. When we hit Greenwood, I'll be more discreet."

"We're not going to Greenwood," Jim said, from the back seat.

"Uh, Jim, we had a deal," Charlie said.

"And I've helped you win at every track along the way. Mohawk, Flamboro, Woodbine. And you haven't exactly taken the straightest route to Toronto. Well, now we're here, and Sick Kids is closer to us than Greenwood. I want to see my daughter, Charlie. Now."

Sick Kids was The Hospital for Sick Children, where Anne was being treated.

"C'mon, Jimbo. Just one more track," Charlie pleaded.

"Daddy, that's not fair."

"Now don't you start," Charlie said.

"Sick Kids. *Now*, Charlie," Jim repeated.

Charlie looked at Brighid. She had her arms folded. "All right," he said with a sigh. He checked out Jim again in the rear view mirror, this time with his sparkly vision. Jim sat there like a human black hole, not a sparkle, not a photon of light escaping him. Charlie tried to imagine the cancer being sucked out of Anne and into that blackness. But as he looked at that dark figure, all he could think was that Charlie the Pearl had a whole bunch of bad luck riding in his back seat.

Brighid sat in the parents' lounge at Sick Kids beside Charlie, wishing she were somewhere else. The place was pleasant enough, with soft lighting and lots of alcoves with comfy chairs. But crying too often tinged the hushed conversations here, and hospitals reminded Brighid of her mom's last days. Worse, having Charlie beside her now just made her dwell on how he hadn't been there at the end when they'd needed him.

She looked at Charlie. She hadn't talked to him since they'd left Jim alone with Anne, hopefully to work his strange magic on his daughter. The early thrill of being on the road and finally getting to know her father had faded like a long shot in the stretch as they'd hit track after track on their way to Toronto. All Charlie seemed to care about now was winning money, cashing in on Jim's bad luck. The more she saw of her dad, the more she wished that she'd been left with her childhood fantasies of him as a romantic gypsy wanderer.

"Anne looked pretty rough," Charlie said finally. "Was… was Mom that bad?"

"Worse," she said quietly. "Near the end." They fell silent again. "Think he can save her?" she asked after a while.

Charlie patted the wad of bills in his jacket. "Well, this guy sure makes people around him lucky. But still…" His voice trailed off.

"What?" she asked, suddenly concerned. "So why wouldn't he make Anne lucky too?"

Charlie shrugged. "He might. But I keep wondering why that thing inside him—"

"So now you believe there is a 'thing'?"

"Starting too. And I keep wondering why it suddenly made it so easy for us to get him here."

Jim came into the lounge before she could consider that. She got up and gave him a big hug. "So, all fixed?" she asked. "Did you pull all the bad stuff out of Anne?"

Jim hesitated. "I don't know," he said, and Brighid felt a chill down her spine. "I held her hand, and I could feel the bad luck in her, like something dirty. And I could feel this thing inside me wanting it. But it was…different. Normally I feel it feed, as if some part of me is filling up. But I couldn't feel that this time."

Brighid shot Charlie a worried look. "Well, you probably took it all out," Brighid said, trying her best to sound hopeful. "You're just too stressed to have felt it flow into you."

Jim nodded slowly. "Maybe you're right. I am beat." He ran a hand through his hair. "Can we find a hotel now? I'm coming back first thing tomorrow to see if she's improved."

"Sure," Brighid said, and hooked her arm through his as they walked to the street.

"What?" Charlie called after them. "Nobody wants to hit the track?"

But the next day brought no improvement in Anne, nor did the day after, nor the day after that. By the end of the week, Charlie noticed that even Brighid was struggling to be positive. The three of them sat picking at breakfast in a little café off Elizabeth Street behind the hospital.

Charlie was reading the newspaper, or rather a racing form hidden inside it. He'd realized the second day of Jim's vigil that he didn't have to take Jim to the track to still cash in on the good luck he created. Charlie had been phoning in winning bets all week to Louie, his bookie of many years. And if the theory that he'd formed this past week about the thing that Jim carried inside him was correct, then Charlie was running out of time to build up Brighid's nest egg. Every bet counted.

Jim looked even worse than when they'd first met. "I don't understand," he said, his eyes sunken and hollow from no sleep. "Why won't it feed from her?"

Charlie sighed and put down his paper. "Because, my bad luck friend, it's feeding from *you*." They both looked at him. "Look, I've been thinking," he said. "If this 'thing' inside you really feeds on bad luck in other people, it must be getting pretty hungry, with you sitting in a private hospital room all week with no bad luck to feed on except Anne's—and yet it still doesn't want hers."

Brighid frowned. "So what are you saying?"

"I think that pulling bad luck into Jim is just a means to an end for this thing. A way to create what it really feeds on."

"Which is?" she asked.

"Think cause and effect," Charlie said. "We found Jim because of the good luck effect around him caused by the bad luck getting sucked into him. But that's just a *side* effect. It's not the real effect this thing wants."

"So what does it want?" Brighid asked.

Charlie looked at Jim, for the first time feeling real compassion. "Think it through. This thing lives *inside* Jim. This thing lives on what all that bad luck creates *inside* him."

"Pain," Jim whispered, a sad understanding dawning in his eyes.

Charlie nodded. "Pain of the person it inhabits. Bad luck creates that pain, and I think that's what it really feeds on."

"That's why I was never able to kill myself. It wants me alive—so I keep suffering," Jim said.

"So why'd it let us bring him to Anne?" Brighid asked. "Not seeing her was causing him pain."

"Not as much as finally letting him come here," Charlie said. "This trip took away the last thing Jim had."

"Hope," Brighid said, a look of horror on her face. "Hope for Anne."

"She's going to die," Jim said, his voice barely a whisper. "She's going to die, and I can't stop it."

Brighid put her arm around him. "No, she isn't! Don't give up. We'll figure out what to do. Won't we, Daddy?"

Charlie had already figured out what to do. Anne couldn't be saved, and neither could Jim. He hadn't shared the rest of his theory—that once Anne was dead, the thing inside Jim would have only one more meal of pain that it could take from Jim—his own death. Charlie figured he had only a few days left to build a nest egg for Brighid.

"Sure," Charlie said. "We'll figure out something, Jimbo." He started reading again.

Suddenly, Brighid reached across the table and pulled the paper down. She stared at the racing form, then at Charlie. "I don't believe you, Daddy. How could you?" she said. She stood up. "Come on, Jim. We'll figure out a way to save Anne. By ourselves." She shot Charlie a final look as they left the restaurant. Her eyes were wet.

Charlie almost ran after her then, to explain why his bets were important, why he had to try to win as much as he could while they had Jim with them. To explain that he was doing this for her, so she could be safe, so she could have a decent life, not a life on the road.

Jim was doomed. She wasn't.

But it was almost post time for the first race. Watching them go, he used a pay phone in the corner to call Louie with his bets before Jim and his lucky influence got too far away.

Charlie spent the day phoning in bets on races. Late afternoon, he walked back to the Strathcona Hotel where the three of them were staying. He was just approaching the front entrance when the doors opened, and out strode Eddie Fenton.

Charlie had no time to run and nowhere to run to. Eddie was turning his way. He'd see Charlie in the next heartbeat.

A car horn blared behind Eddie. Eddie spun around, swearing at the driver as the car sped past. Seizing his chance, Charlie slipped into the hotel unnoticed and watched from inside as Eddie, oblivious to the proximity of his old mentor, disappeared up the street.

Charlie let out his breath, shaken by the near miss. He'd been lucky. He stopped.

Lucky.

He laughed. Of course he'd been lucky. Jim had sucked all the bad luck out of him. He could probably walk right up to Eddie and tweak his nose, and Eddie still wouldn't see him. Feeling invincible, Charlie bounded up the stairs to their rooms.

Still, no use taking chances. Charlie made some phone calls to friends on Charlie's side of the law and got the scoop on Eddie. Eddie was out on bail, the money put up by some very dangerous people that Eddie was now working for, fixing second and third card boxing matches in New York State.

Footsteps passed by in the hall. A key turned, and the door next to Charlie's opened and closed. That was Jim's room. The walls were paper thin, and Charlie could hear the murmurs of a whispered conversation. Jim and Brighid? Where had they been all day? And why were they whispering? Suspicious, Charlie got up quietly and put a glass to the wall to listen.

He didn't listen long. Dropping the glass, he rushed next door and burst into the room.

"Are you out of your mind?" Charlie yelled at Brighid. "You're going to *kill* him?"

Brighid and Jim sat on the edge of Jim's bed, a study in opposites. Brighid sat bolt upright, a young woman wise beyond her years, her face determined, her eyes meeting Charlie's and not wavering. Jim sat slumped and shrunken, a man old before his time, eyes downcast, no fight left in him. Between them lay a gun.

"It's the only way to save Anne, Charlie," Brighid said.

Charlie noted that she wasn't calling him 'Daddy' anymore. "How can you know that?"

"You told us," Brighid said.

"*I* told you!?"

"This thing in me needs my pain," Jim whispered. "And Anne's the only way it can still hurt me. The doctors say she should be responding. This thing is killing her. But if I'm dead, the thing will have no reason for her to die. She'll recover." He looked up at Charlie. "She's all I've got."

"And Bee's all *I've* got. And you want to make her a murderer," Charlie snarled, advancing on him, a rare anger rising in him.

Brighid stepped between them. "It's not murder. Jim *wants* to die."

"*You* would still be taking a life."

"I'll die soon anyway," Jim said. "I can feel it. But this thing won't let me die until Anne does, until it gets that last meal of pain from me."

"And this way, Anne lives," Brighid said. "So what are we doing that's wrong, Charlie?"

"You're killing a man!"

"A man who makes you a lot of money? Is that it?"

"That's not fair, Bee. I'm only thinking of us."

"*Us*? When did you ever think of *us*, Charlie? Where were you all my life? Where were you when mom was dying like Anne's dying?"

"Is that what this is about?" Charlie shouted, his shame and guilt feeding his anger. "This isn't going to bring your mom back, Bee."

She slapped him then, hard, and that slap carried every bit of pain that Charlie had ever felt in his life. He stared at her dumbstruck, rubbing his cheek. "Fuck you, Charlie," she sobbed, tears streaming down her face.

They stood there, father and daughter, two strangers, close enough to hold each other, but suddenly further apart than a lifetime of separate lives had ever made them. Shaken as he'd never been before, Charlie slumped down on the opposite bed. Brighid did the same. Silence fell on the room as heavy as a bust card on a blackjack table.

Finally, Charlie spoke, his voice flat and empty. "I'll take you away from here, from him."

"I'll run away," she replied, her voice cold and hard. "I'll come back."

"I'll take that gun."

"We'll get another. Or find another way."

He looked at her. She wouldn't meet his eyes. "It doesn't matter what I say, does it?" he asked. She shook her head, still not looking at him. Charlie sighed. Before either of them could stop him, he reached over and grabbed the gun. "Well, I won't let you do this."

"Fuck, Charlie," Brighid swore. "Haven't you heard anything—"

"No," he said. "I mean, I won't let my daughter do this." He turned to Jim, the gun as cold in his hand as dice on a losing streak. "So, my sad friend," he said, his voice barely a whisper, not believing he was having this conversation, "exactly where in this beautiful city would you like to die?"

They decided on the Toronto Islands. Charlie took the Ward's Island ferry, while Jim took the ferry to Centre Island an hour later. They met at Hanlan's Point just before midnight. The beach was deserted, and a half moon over the lake gave them enough light to make their way to a small stand of trees.

Jim had written a suicide note. The plan was for Jim to hold the gun, and Charlie to pull the trigger. "Don't get your hopes up, Jimbo," Charlie said as Jim knelt down. "I doubt this will be any more effective than when you tried it yourself. That thing inside you will probably still make the gun misfire."

Jim shrugged. "Let's hope you're wrong."

Charlie was desperately hoping he was right. Because he really didn't want to kill a man. Plus if this didn't work, he'd be able to get a few more bets down before Jim really was gone, but still show Brighid that he'd tried to help save Anne.

"Anyway," Jim said, "we'll soon find out." He took out the gun and put it to his head.

Charlie slipped his shaking hand over Jim's and his finger over the trigger. "Anything you want to say?"

Jim thought a moment. "Just thanks. And look after Anne." He paused. "That's all." He smiled as Charlie slowly squeezed the trigger.

The gun fired.

Jim died.

And Charlie's life changed forever.

Charlie's first clue that something was very, very wrong came when he missed the ferry back and had to wait an hour for the next one. That just didn't seem lucky to Charlie, but he figured that his streak was ending now that Jim was gone. His second clue came when the bad feeling in his gut didn't go away.

That bad feeling had hit him the moment after Jim had died. At the time, he'd figured that it was simply the kind of bad feeling that good people got when they had just done something very wrong, like killing a man. An hour later, he wasn't so sure. An hour later, he was thinking that this was more the kind of bad feeling that came from having something inside of you that you'd rather have on the outside.

His final clue came on the ferry ride back when he noticed that the lighting seemed wrong. It was brighter than it should be. Trembling, Charlie looked at his fellow passengers in the special way he had, kind of sideways, at an angle. All the people around him were very, very…

Sparkly.

Charlie made his way to the rail and threw up over the side. He watched his vomit on the waves slide behind the ferry, his dreams slipping away like a horse left at the post. He stared down, the dark water below mirroring the darkness he now felt inside, the darkness of the thing that had lived inside Jim.

The thing that was now inside Charlie.

Charlie didn't tell Brighid. He figured that he could still make this work for them. What did it matter if Charlie the Pearl was now unluckier than a man betting black on a roulette wheel with nothing but red. Brighid was with him and would therefore be as lucky as she'd been around Jim. Charlie would just have her place all of their bets.

But the thing inside him had other plans.

"So ends a perfect day," Brighid said, as they sat in the stands at Greenwood watching their horse cross the finish line dead last in the tenth race. "We lost every race." She tore up their tickets and tossed them in the air with a whoop. "Well, Daddy, I'd say our winning streak is over."

"You're awfully cheery about it," Charlie said, feeling the thing inside him sucking in bad luck from the people around him. It felt like having his stomach pumped in reverse. At least, Brighid was calling him 'Daddy' again.

She shrugged. "Hey, we saved Anne. Her doctors called her recovery a miracle. And what do two top con artists like us need with luck, anyway?" she said with a grin. Then she frowned. "Besides, that luck thing with Jim? I never liked it. It just never felt good."

"I just wanted to give you a life, Bee," he said. "Make a nest egg for you."

"And all I *ever* wanted," Brighid said, "was to get to know my father. Which I now plan to do." She hugged him and turned back to watch the horses file off the track.

He looked at her. His beautiful girl. Best thing he'd ever done with his life was making her. Maybe she was right. Maybe nothing had really changed. Maybe they could make a life together on the road. Maybe…

His throat constricted as something caught his eye. "Bee," he said quietly, "when did you get that lump on your neck?"

♣

The doctors said all the things that doctors say in those situations. Things about new drugs and the latest procedures. About Brighid being young and strong. About catching it early. But Charlie could read people, and he read in their faces all the things that they weren't telling him.

His daughter was going to die.

Charlie sat in the hall outside Brighid's ward, his face in his hands. He should have figured it out earlier. This thing inside him now lived on his misery and pain, so it had to attack his happiness the same way it had attacked Jim's. And Brighid was the key to Charlie's happiness.

Charlie's love for his daughter was killing her. No, he thought bitterly. His greed was killing her. He'd started out chasing the lucky town because Charlie the Pearl wanted the big score. And it had led them here.

He sat there, cursing Jim and the day he'd found him. Jim had escaped his misery by passing it on to Charlie, saving his own daughter by condemning Brighid. Now Charlie was in exactly the same spot.

He sat up. Exactly the same spot. So that meant…

A smile spread slowly across his face. It took him a few minutes to run through all the angles in his head, making sure he wasn't overlooking something. Finding a pay phone near the elevator, he dropped in a quarter and dialed. "Strathcona Hotel? Great. I want to leave a message for one of your guests, a Mister Eddie Fenton. No, just say it's from a friend. Here's the message."

He hung up and made another call, this time to Louie, his bookie. Charlie had used Louie for many years and knew he could be trusted to payoff on a winner. Even a very big winner. Louie happily took Charlie's bets. "Lots of action from the wise guys on the favorites on those cards, Charlie," Louie said. "Thought I was going to have to lay some of it off until you called."

Charlie hung up. He just had one more thing left to do.

Charlie stood by Brighid's bed. "It was never about the money, Bee," he explained to her. "It was always about you. A dad like me might not be around come tomorrow, and I needed to know that you'd be taken care of, that you'd have enough no matter what this world threw at you." He wiped away tears. "Just wanted you to know that."

Brighid didn't say anything because she was asleep when Charlie said those things because Charlie knew he wouldn't have been able to say goodbye when she was awake. He kissed her pale brow, and left a letter by her bedside, in which he provided an excellent explanation of what she must do when she opened that letter, and a much less satisfactory explanation, in his mind, of just how much she meant to Charlie and how much he loved her and how proud he was of her.

Then Charlie left to keep an appointment that he'd made, happy in the knowledge that right to the end, even with all the bad luck in the world riding around inside him, it still didn't pay to bet against Charlie the Pearl.

♣

The midway at the Canadian National Exhibition was jammed with parents trailing kids gorging themselves on candy floss, older kids sucking on orange or grape Lolas, and teenage boys trying to win their girlfriends a stuffed animal at one of the games.

Charlie leaned against the wooden frame of the Flyer, just taking it all in. Above him, the roller coaster clanked and rattled its way up the climb to its first plunge. Behind the Flyer, the Shell Tower rose over the park and the midway.

Across from him sat the freak sideshow. A carnie stood at a raised ticket booth beside the entrance. The man was dressed in a white tux with a matching white top hat, and was exhorting passersby, in a voice that would not have been out of place on the stage in Stratford, to "Enter and be amazed! See Dainty Dora, the fat woman. Marvel at the Snake Man. Gasp at the Dog-faced Boy!"

Charlie smiled, remembering again his years as a carnie, years that had been his happiest. He remembered, too, that day that he'd brought Brighid here for one of the best days of his life. All of those things had made this as good a place as any for what Charlie had planned.

He took one last look around. He never had to look at this world in any special way. These places, they always looked the same to him.

Sparkly.

Not so much because he was seeing luck on the people or the places. Mostly, Charlie always figured, because he had always felt lucky just to be here.

Eddie found him there at ten o'clock, because that was where Charlie's anonymous message to Eddie had said Charlie would be at ten o'clock. Charlie pretended to be surprised. He let Eddie prod him along the midway with the gun in his pocket, between the Horse Palace and the Coliseum, through the north parking lot and across the train tracks under the Gardiner Expressway, until he pulled Charlie into the shadows there and proceeded to beat the crap out of him.

"Did ya think you could do that to me, old man?" Eddie snarled as he kicked Charlie again. "Did ya think I wouldn't get you?"

"I hear you're into fixing fights, Eddie," Charlie managed to say, when Eddie paused to catch his breath.

Eddie stopped. "That's right. And making big money."

Charlie spat out a tooth. "Doing it smart, too, I hear. Picking fights off the main card. Fix it so the favorite wins. No big underdog but still good odds. Attracts less attention from the boxing commission."

Eddie laughed. "Yeah. You taught me something after all."

"Oh, I'm not sure about that. Me? I bet on all the underdogs tonight. Better odds."

"Yeah? Well, that makes you a loser in more ways than one, old man," Eddie said, taking out his gun and pointing it at Charlie's head.

Charlie felt the thing that lived inside him now, hovering just behind his eyes, ready to leap when the bullet hit.

Just as it had leaped to Jim from the other driver in that car crash. Just as it had leaped to Charlie when Jim died. Ready to leap.

Leap to Eddie.

Charlie twisted his head around to smile up past the barrel of the gun at Eddie.

"Care to place a little bet on that, kid?"

Eddie stared down at Charlie's body. He felt different. He felt bad. Not the kind of bad that good people feel when they realize they have done something terribly wrong, like killing a man in cold blood, but the kind of bad that Eddie sometimes felt when he ate leftover pizza. The kind of bad that came from having something inside of him that he'd rather have on the outside.

But Eddie was a tough guy, so he shrugged it off, turned his back on Charlie's corpse, and returned to his car. Only his car wasn't there.

Cursing his luck and car thieves everywhere, Eddie walked back to his apartment, finding himself suddenly and strangely invisible to taxis and bus drivers. Once home, he tuned his TV into the fights and plopped down on his worn sofa with a beer to enjoy the predetermined outcomes.

Outcomes that turned out, one after another to Eddie's growing panic, to be less predetermined than Eddie had expected.

The men who lost money on Eddie's supposedly fixed fights were not the sort of people who liked to lose money on supposedly fixed fights. They found Eddie, surprising-ly easily despite his best efforts to hide, and removed certain body parts of which Eddie had been rather fond. They left Eddie to die, but as luck would have it—all bad from Eddie's point of view—he didn't.

Instead, the police found him and took him to hospital. When he recovered, they charged him with the murder of a man shot three times in an alley earlier that month. Later still, they charged him with the murder of Charles Tobias Perlman. The arresting detective told reporters that only an amazing series of lucky breaks had enabled them to tie both killings to Eddie.

The first thing Brighid's doctors told her when she woke up was that the remission of her cancer was a miracle and that she was very lucky to be alive. The second thing they told her, when she asked about Charlie, was that her father had left an envelope for her.

Brighid wondered why Charlie wasn't there himself, but she followed the instructions in his letter exactly as he'd laid them out.

She called a man named Louie who explained to her that her father had placed several large winning bets on her behalf on every second and third card boxing match in Buffalo earlier that week. How large? she asked. Very large, he said. Brighid sat down suddenly when Louie told her how much she had won.

But it wasn't until later that night, after the police had called her, and she stood crying in the morgue as she identified Charlie's body, that she found out how much she had also lost.

♣

One year later, Brighid strolled down the midway at the Ex. She watched the big Ferris wheel slowly turning, smelled the candy floss, listened to the screams from the roller-coaster and the cries of the barkers, remembering that day as a child here with Charlie. She remembered too Charlie saying that his days as a carnie had been his happiest ever.

Walking up to one of the carnies, she gave him a sign that Charlie had taught her. "So," she said when he returned it. "You hiring?"

The next day, on one of her breaks from running the ring toss game, she sat down beside another carnie, a grizzled veteran named Hank. He nodded at her. "Hear you're gonna be hitting the road with us. Most o' you kids, you just do this show. Get your cash then you're back to school come fall."

Brighid nodded. "I'm taking a year off before I start university. I'm writing a book."

"A book?" he said, squinting one eyed at her.

"Yep," she said, pulling a battered journal and pen from her backpack. "That's why I want to talk to you."

He looked puzzled. "Me? Why me?"

She grinned. "Cuz I understand you knew my father."

Later that day, her journal guarding the tales that the carnies had told her of Charlie, Brighid stopped in the center of the midway on her way back to her last shift. Slowly, she turned around and around, trying to take it all in, trying to look at the carnival the way Charlie had said that he looked for luck in life.

Sideways. Kind of at an angle.

It took a moment, but it came. She smiled. The big wheel, the coaster, the lights, the games, the crowd. All of it. Every crass, corny bit of it. It all looked the same.

Sparkly.

"Thanks, Daddy," she whispered. "I think I finally found you after all."

Story Notes

The genesis for this story came from the Bruce Springsteen song, "Lucky Town," and also another song from the Boss, "Local Hero," from the same album. I wanted to write a song about a con man and gambler ever since I heard those songs, and at some point the opening lines to this story came into my head. Then I just needed to figure out Charlie's story —a story that just wasn't coming together until I added his daughter. After that, Charlie, Brighid, and the story all had a goal to aim for, which made it easier for all of us.

This was the first of a planned series of stories that I am writing that are loosely based on or inspired by Springsteen songs. Another you can look for is "Radio Nowhere," which appeared in the anthology *Campus Chills* and is available as a stand-alone ebook.

About
the Author

"One of Canada's most original writers of speculative fiction."   —*Library Journal*

"A great storyteller with a gifted and individual voice."   —*Charles de Lint*

Douglas Smith is an award-winning Canadian author who has been published in thirty countries and twenty-five languages.

His works include the novel, *The Wolf at the End of the World*, an urban fantasy with shapeshifters and Cree and Ojibwe mythology, and the collections *Chimerascope* (2010), *Impossibilia* (2008), and *La Danse des Esprits* (France, 2011).

Doug has won Canada's Aurora Award three times, and has been a finalist for the John W. Campbell Award, CBC's Bookies Award, Canada's juried Sunburst Award, and France's juried Prix Masterton and Prix Bob Morane.

His website is smithwriter.com, and he tweets at twitter.com/smithwritr. You can subscribe to Doug's mailing list at www.smithwriter.com/mailing_list and contact Doug at www.smithwriter.com/contact.

Bonus Section

Chimerascope
© Douglas Smith

Sunburst Award finalist
Aurora Award finalist
CBC's Bookies Award finalist

Chimerascope [ki-meer-uh-skohp]—a story of many
parts…

Doug's second collection contains sixteen of his best stories, including an award winner, a Best New Horror selection, and eight award finalists. Stories of fantasy and science
fiction that take you from love in fourteenth-century Japan
to humanity's last stand, from virtual reality to the end
of reality, from alien drug addictions to a dinner where a
man loses everything.

"His stories are a treasure trove of riches that will touch your heart while making you think."
                    —*Robert J. Sawyer, Hugo Award-winning author*

"A massively enjoyable trek…all filtered through Smith's remarkable imagination and prodigious talent."
                    —*Quill and Quire* (starred review)

"The 16 stories in this collection showcase the inventive mind and immense storytelling talent of one of Canada's most original writers of speculative fiction."
                    —*Library Journal*

"An entertaining selection of stories that deftly span multiple genres."   —*Publishers Weekly*

"An engaging and entertaining volume, pieces of whose content resonate after the book is finished."   —*Booklist*

"Douglas Smith is an extraordinary author whom every lover of quality speculative fiction should read. Rating: A+"
                    —*Fantasy Book Critic*

"Arrestingly inventive premises in a field where really interesting new ideas are harder and harder to find. …Smith is definitely an author who deserves to be more widely read."
                    —*Strange Horizons*

"A beautifully diverse selection of short tales…well-crafted, easily digestible; several of the stories are incredibly moving and stick with the reader long after."
                    —*Sunburst Award jury*

"Smith is a master of beginnings…some of the most well-crafted hooks you'll find anywhere…[with] endings that feel satisfying and right." —*Canadian Science Fiction Review*

For more, please see the collection *Chimerascope*.

[novel excerpt]

The Wolf At The End Of The World
© Douglas Smith
Introduction by World Fantasy Award winner, Charles de Lint

Author's note: The Wolf at the End of the World *takes place five years after the events in Doug's award-winning novelette, "Spirit Dance" (available in his earlier collection,* Impossibilia, *or as a stand-alone ebook). In the novel, Gwyn Blaidd, the hero of "Spirit Dance," battles ancient native spirits, the shadowy Tainchel, and his own dark past in a race to solve a murder that might mean the end of the world. If you enjoyed "Spirit Dance," here's your chance to continue your journey with Gwyn, Ed, Leiddia, Mitch, and a host of new characters.*

CHAPTER 1

MARY

Everything had gone wrong, and now Mary Two Rivers was running away. Away from the dam site, away from the damage they'd done, stumbling through the bush in the dark, trying to keep up with Jimmy White Creek and ahead of the security guards. And the dogs. She could hear dogs barking now.

What had she been thinking? Why had she gone along with Jimmy and the rest of them? She was an A student. She was going to university in the fall. She had plans, plans to get off the Rez. Plans that didn't include jail.

Hanging a banner over the dam to protest the loss of Ojibwe land was one thing, but then somebody had poured gasoline on one of the construction vehicles and lit it on fire. And she'd let herself be part of it.

Just because Jimmy had a cute smile and cuter butt—a butt that was getting farther and farther ahead of her as she struggled to keep up. She was a bookworm, not an athlete, and the ground was starting to rise. Jimmy was heading for the west ridge overlooking the still dormant dam and its reservoir lake. She didn't know where the other kids were. Everyone had scattered when the guards appeared, and she'd followed Jimmy. Or tried to.

"Jimmy!" she cried in a desperate whisper. "Wait up!" She didn't know these woods anymore. If she lost him, she doubted she'd get far before the guards caught her.

Jimmy stopped on the hill ahead of her, chest heaving, breath hanging misty in the chill October air. The moonlight caught his pale, sweating face, and in that moment, she wondered how she'd ever thought he was handsome. "Mary, you gotta keep up," he panted, his voice breaking. "There's a path through the trees on top of the ridge. We'll lose them in there and cut back to the Rez." He started up the slope again, not waiting for her.

Forcing her trembling legs to move, she kept climbing. Jimmy disappeared over the top. Half a minute later, she scrambled up the last few yards. She looked around. Jimmy was nowhere in sight.

The tall jack pines stood closer here, the undergrowth thick between them, their high tops touching, blocking off the cold light from the waxing half moon. Whatever path Jimmy had taken was invisible, hidden by darkness.

She was alone and lost.

She sank to the ground, shaking. She was going to be caught. She was going to jail. What would her parents say? Their dream was for her to get a degree, to beat the odds of being born on the Rez. Their dream…

She swore softly to herself. *Her* dream, too. She stood up, anger conquering her fear. They would *not* catch her. Sucking in a deep breath, she let it out slowly to calm herself as she looked back down the hill she'd just climbed.

The dam and its dark captured lake lay in the distance below. Five burly figures were climbing the bottom of the hill. But worse, ahead of the guards, two gray shadows leapt over the rocks and brush of the slope. The dogs would reach her in less than a minute.

Turning back to the forest, she listened for any sound of Jimmy running ahead. *There.* Had that been a branch snapping deep in the woods? She moved in the direction of the noise, tripping over unseen rocks and roots. One patch of darkness loomed blacker than the rest. She stepped closer. It seemed to be an opening through the trees. Praying for this to be the path that Jimmy had taken, she plunged ahead.

As she moved into the forest, her eyes slowly adjusted to the deeper darkness under the trees, aided by the occasional sliver of moonlight slicing through the canopy of branches above. This was definitely a path. She paused a moment, straining to hear any sound of pursuit. The dogs were still barking, but they didn't sound any closer.

The barking stopped. In the sudden silence, she heard the yip of a fox. She shuddered, remembering a saying of her *misoomish*, her grandfather. "Bad luck," he'd told her as a child. "You hear a fox bark in the night, that's bad luck." But then the dogs took up their call again, and she allowed herself a small thrill of hope. The barking was fainter now. The dogs, and presumably the men with them, were moving away from her. They hadn't found this path.

She was going to get away. The tension gripping her vanished, and her shaking legs gave way. She collapsed onto the soft cushion of pine needles that covered the ground, sweat soaking her t-shirt under her parka. She hugged her knees to her chest, shivering from the chill and the adrenaline still in her.

Now that the immediate danger was gone, another thought came to her. Just last week, a worker had died at the dam site. Animal attack, the cops had said. She swallowed. Because his body had been partially eaten.

Suddenly, huddled on the forest floor in the dark, she didn't feel quite as safe as she had a moment before. She wanted nothing more than to be home in her own bed, to hear her parents in the next room, talking or arguing, she didn't care which, just so long as she was out of this nightmare. With that image filling her heart, she stood and started along the path once more, still praying to catch Jimmy, to have him lead her out of these woods, to lead her home.

A brightness grew ahead. A few seconds later, she stepped into a clearing lit in cold luminescence by the half moon above and enclosed by high rock walls ahead and to her left. To her right, the clearing gave way to the pines again, the level ground sloping away sharply. She walked to the top of the slope, looking for a way down. Her heart fell.

Halfway down, the pines thinned and then disappeared completely where the forest had been cleared near the bottom. The slope ended at the road leading onto the top of the dam. Beyond the dam, the black surface of the lake rippled like some great beast shuddering itself awake in the night.

She'd run the wrong way, back toward the dam.

With a sudden sick feeling, she realized what she should have figured out earlier. The dogs would have followed a scent. They hadn't followed her, so they must have been on Jimmy's trail, which meant Jimmy had taken another path, not the one that had led her here.

She'd taken the wrong path.

She looked around the clearing, searching for some alternative to retracing her steps. The slope below led right back to the dam and the scene of the crime, so that route was out. The dark lake caught her attention again, recalling childhood memories of her grandfather's stories, the ones about the evil spirits that lived in deep water.

She turned her back on the lake and those memories. Enough. Time to go home. She considered the rock walls rising above her. The one facing the entrance to the path was almost sheer and rose too high for her even to think of trying to scale it. The wall facing the lake was less steep and offered some handholds for climbing.

It looked about twenty feet high. She examined its face for the best route, finally selecting a path that would bring her up beside a large boulder perched by itself at the top of the wall.

Or maybe it was a bush, since she saw something move on it, like branches shifting in the wind. Just then, a cloud scuttled across the night sky, swallowing the moon. As the clearing fell dark, she shivered at a sudden strange thought—that the shape had resembled something crouched there, and what she'd seen moving were actually long locks of hair.

Another gust brought a smell down to her, thick and heavy—the smell of mushrooms and rotting wood and wet moss. Bitter, and yet, at the same time, so sickly sweet she thought she would retch.

The cloud hiding the moon moved on. Pale moonlight shone down again, cold and cruel, and Mary finally saw what crouched above her, waiting.

Look for *The Wolf at the End of the World* at all major book retailers in 2013